DOUGHBOY CITY
An Occupied Berlin Story

DAVID G. GUERRA

David G. Guerra

DOUGHBOY CITY: an OCCUPIED BERLIN story (Tales from Freedom's Outpost)

Subject headings:

Fiction – Crime
Fiction – Historical (Cold War, 1945 – 1990)
Fiction – Mystery

ISBN: 1494498987
ISBN-13: 978-1494498986

website: http://www.DaveGuerra.com/books/DoughboyCity
blog: OccupiedBerlin.blogspot.com
email: dave@daveguerra.com

Front Cover photo by Charles R. Sledge
(Doughboy and Wire photo used by permission)
Back Cover and design by David G. Guerra.

First Printing: 2014
10 9 8 7 6 5 4 3 2 1

DEDICATION

To My Wife and Children
You are my inspiration

CONTENTS

Acknowledgments   viii

Chapter One   1

Chapter Two   5

Chapter Three   9

Chapter Four   14

Chapter Five   18

Chapter Six   23

Chapter Seven   30

Chapter Eight   34

Chapter Nine   39

Chapter Ten   47

Chapter Eleven   54

Chapter Twelve   57

Chapter Thirteen   60

Chapter Fourteen   63

Chapter Fifteen   67

Chapter Sixteen   73

Chapter Seventeen   76

Chapter Eighteen   81

Chapter Nineteen   84

Chapter Twenty   87

DAVID G. GUERRA

Chapter Twenty-One   90

Chapter Twenty-Two   95

Epilogue   100

About The Author   102

ACKNOWLEDGMENTS

Words can express only so much about how I feel about the people who helped me throughout the entire process. The roots of this book can be traced back to the day I stepped off that Pan Am flight from New York to Berlin on November 1, 1985. While there are so many individuals and organizations I must thank I just cannot mention everyone so please forgive me.

The biggest thanks go to my wife, Teresa, my children, Emma and Matthew, and my Mother and Brothers. You will never know how much your support means to me.

Thank You to every Soldier and Airman that served with the U.S. Army's Berlin Brigade (1945-1994). It is an honor to have served and be associated with such great Soldiers, Airmen, and Leaders.

Very Special Thanks to those who served with me in 3rd Platoon, Alpha Company, 6th Battalion, 502nd Infantry. Especially to Farrell, Steve, and Dan, you are the brothers that I would have gone through hell and back, no questions asked. Thanks.

Thank you to the citizens of West Berlin, Germany. From 1945 to 1990, you never lost hope in what we were doing in Berlin and knowing that you were right there next to us the entire time made our unique bond that very extraordinary. Vielen Dank!

A Big Thanks to Charles R. Sledge for the last minute assistance. For anyone who I have failed to mention and has been with me over the years, I ask your forgiveness. Whether you know it or not, you have truly helped me every step of the way.

Thank You,
Dave

DAVID G. GUERRA

CHAPTER ONE

*1st Belorussian Front • 1st Guards Tank Army • 197th Light Artillery
Brigade • 7th Mortar Battalion • April 20 1945 • 0445hrs •
Jühnsdorf, Germany (15km north of Zossen, Germany)*

"Anatoly…Anatoly, wake up. It is time to move."

"Again?" a young battle hardened ефрейтор (Efreitor) Anatoly
Prevelov asks from under the only thing that he can still claim as his since
the Great Patriotic War began over a lifetime ago, his wool blanket.

"Yes, again!" another even younger looking and just as battle hardened
Private Yuri Baseliv responds with just as much frustration as his friend
since the first day they met for basic Mortar Training over a year ago. Has it
really been that long?

Their training began almost one month after the end of the Battle of
Stalingrad where both had arrived on the train to the outskirts of the city to
find that only the dead Nazi's were left in the city. Finding themselves with
little to do among a sea of surviving "draftees" they raised their hands when
the word came down for volunteers to the artillery corps. That was to be
their reward for the faithful service to Mother Russia! That mattered little to
everyone that raised their hand. All that mattered to them was that the
Artillery Corps would mean that they would not be on the front lines.

Their train of thought was that Artillery was always behind, sometimes
over the horizon from the battle lines. It was a relatively safe place. At least,
that is what the late comers thought. About 60 of the soldiers that raised
their hands became Artillery soldiers that afternoon.

It was when the Training Sergeant lined everyone up and counted 1, 2, 3
and pointed to one soldier at a time as he counted that the mortar team was

created. Yuri, Anatoly, and Pyotr Jemmovich made Mortar Crew 16.

"Since Warsaw that is all we do…move…move again…and more moving", mumbled Anatoly as he starts to roll his blanket and proceeds to stuff it into his pack.

"Yes. I like that we are moving it means that we will be home soon!"

"Do you really think that Comrade Basilev?"

"Of course, I think so! Why would they not want to let us go home after we have defeated the National Socialists?"

"Yuri, do you remember what the good Party Officer told us at the last meeting before crossing into this forsaken country? He said the war was but a small struggle for the future of the Soviet Union. Remember, how he painted the picture of life after this Great Patriotic War. It will be another struggle but it will be better for all of us but before we can parade in front of the Kremlin, we must win this war and defeat Germany."

"Always the pessimist. You are reading between lines that are not there." Yuri fired back as he secured his equipment on the trailer that is carrying their mortar tube, baseplate, and ammunition, "Are you almost ready?"

April 21 1945 • 1507hrs • Kleinbeeren, Germany (10km north of Jühnsdorf, Germany)

"Well, where are we?" looking to the passenger door as it opens and Yuri starts to climb in.

"I just heard the Lieutenant tell Sergeant Feskov that when the sun goes down look to the north we will see lights. The lights will be that of the fires and what electricity is available in the city. The light will be bright because we are close." Pyotr Jemmovich, speaks with such a matter of fact in his voice. He too will be glad when this is over.

"But where are we, Pyotr"

"We are close, very close. Feskov said we will get new maps in the morning."

"We do not need a map, we have a spotter. Do we still have one?"

"If the spotter that you refer to is the one that we passed just west of Guldendorf after we crossed the Oder River?"

"Yes…"

"He has a faster vehicle that is if it still works. And yes he is still alive but he better stay fast. I hate firing blind, especially when the Infantry calls for fire. You know those Infantry Lieutenants cannot read a map to save their lives."

"Oh yes, I agree. Luckily, there has not been a repeat of that fiasco."

"Yes, we have learned so much since that day." Yuri reassures his friend that the deadly accidental fratricide incident west of Guldendorf will never be repeated. If that Infantry officer had remained calm under fire, he would have known that he was calling for a High Explosive Ammunition Mortar attack on his own position as well as the position of all the men in his platoon.

Anatoly sighs as they all remember and pulls out his blanket and uses it as a pillow against the interior doorframe. He knows it is longer but it seems that just as he shut his eyes someone is banging on the door to wake them up and get ready to move. Again…

April 23 1945 • 1033hrs • Outskirts of Berlin, Germany (3km north of Heinersdorf, Germany)

The battle waged so furious and so fast that Anatoly, Yuri and Pyotr were leaving bundles of mortar rounds behind, as it seemed that as fast as they setup and fired off several rounds of High Explosive, they packed and moved. They were certain the final push into Berlin was on. It never occurred to any of them that at some point someone had to go back and pick up the extra ammo.

A cleanup crew maybe? Surely, the Soviet Military had a unit that collected unexploded devices. Maybe the conquered? Yes, they would be put to work to clean up the mess. Of course, they would be the ones responsible; after all, they created this mess in the first place.

No one worried about that today. Today was about bringing this madness to an end.

For most of the day and evening, the 7th Mortar Battalion spent it crossing what appeared to be the last cultivated field before the houses, buildings, churches, and factories started to appear with greater frequency.

"This is it! This is as close as we can get to Berlin without setting foot in Berlin proper."

"Yuri, what are you talking about?"

"Anatoly, Pyotr look at the map," pointing to a green area on the map south of a canal, marked Тельтов (Teltow) that ran through the southern part of the city from the Гавел (Havel) river, "we are here. When we cross this street [pointing to a street running parallel and south of the canal marked "Восточно-Прусская набережной" (Ostpruessendamm)] we will be in Berlin proper and there is no turning back."

"So it is true, we are almost done here."

"I do not think so Comrade Prevelov."

"OK, Mister Comrade Yuri Baseliv please tell us why you do not think so"

"Look at all the ammunition we were supplied with today. They gave us all that ammo because they want us to use it. They expect heavy fighting. No, no my friends this will be one that will take us past the May Day."

"Yuri, you know what your problem is?" looking Baseliv right in the eye, "You think too much."

"We shall see," said Anatoly as he returned the map back into its case and reaching for his cup of tea.

Baseliv savored the hot tea knowing that once the final push to the city center begins things will most certainly be moving at a much faster pace and steeping hot tea will become a luxury for after the great battle that is yet to unfold. Yes, he knows that once the house-to-house fighting begins the end will be long and arduous to reach.

The following day General Nikolai Erastovich Berzarin's 5th Shock Army and General Mikhail Efimovich Katukov's 1st Guards Tank Army reached the Teltow canal and crossed it. The battle for Berlin had officially begun.

CHAPTER TWO

United States Army • Berlin Brigade • Andrews Barracks •
November 9 1989 • 1545hrs • West Berlin, Germany (110 miles east
of West Germany)

"Why won't anyone believe me?" I asked as two United States Army Criminal Investigation Command (CID) agents were acting as if they were taking my statement. It was not that hard to believe, well at least I did not think it was. My friend was murdered by his Sergeant. OK, I did not actually see the murder take place but I just know that Staff Sergeant Rafael Herndez somehow managed to kill PFC Vela. Don't ask me how I know I just know he did it.

"Specialist Guerra, you can't just come in here and accuse a US Army Non-Commissioned Officer (NCO) of murdering one of his own men," United States Army Criminal Investigation Command Special Agent Manny Emmett said.

I was not naïve to the way the Army did things, I grew up around the military almost all my life. My father was a career Army NCO and now I was an enlisted man, a Specialist (E-4) to be exact. I knew that in both military and civilian life no one could be accused without real proof, real evidence. Yet, I couldn't shake the fact that SSG Herndez did something to make the explosion happen and kill my friend Private First Class (E-3) David Vela.

"Look, Specialist. We cannot just go to your unit with guns blazing and pluck that Staff Sergeant out of the barracks because Specialist E-4 Daniel Guerra said so."

"I know, I know, but I can't buy the 'official story' that Vela accidently hit a couple of old Russian mortar shells with his e-tool and after more than 40 years of laying in the dirt they exploded, killing him."

5

"Guerra, how long have you been in the city?"

"Going on two and a half years." It was actually two years, four months, 27 days, 6 hours, 28 minutes to be exact but who's counting?

"Since then, how many times have you heard the news reports on AFN (Armed Forces Network Radio and Television Service) Berlin of unexploded bombs found in new subway construction or new housing construction in the Zone?"

"Not all the time but I have heard about it happening"

"Well, then you know that in late April 1945 the Soviets threw everything they had into capturing Berlin. Coming in from the south was the Soviet's 1st Ukrainian Army Group under Marshall Georgy Zhukov. Zhukov and his men were moving so fast that they had no time to set up shop and wait for the rest of the Soviets to get to Berlin. It was no secret that Soviets left stuff all along their path from the Oder to the Reichstag. So you see the rounds were just waiting there to be found either by bulldozer, backhoe, or an e-tool."

An Entrenching tool or "E-tool", as we called it, was the soldier's multipurpose tool of its time. It was a shovel, an axe, a close quarter weapon, heck in a pinch, it made latrines.

"I know this, we were all reminded that day at Doughboy City."

"Then explain how did SSG Herndez manage to pick the right spot for Vela to start digging?" asked Agent Emmett.

"I just don't know how," in a near frustrated tone, "but I just know he had something to do with this."

"That's right, you don't know. You want to know what we call it. We call it Bad Luck, coincidence, call it whatever you want to call it but without solid proof there is just nothing we can do. Look, I like you Guerra and I don't want to see anything bad happen to you or your Army career and that's why we are not taking any of this down. Now, this does not mean that I don't respect you and your initiative when it comes to your friend. Hell, I wish I had friends like you. I know I would want someone in my corner questioning the circumstances of my death, when that time comes. I also know that I would not want my friend to start making false accusations because something doesn't smell right."

"Agent Emmett, I understand completely what you are saying and I want someone in my corner when my day comes but someone not so long ago said, 'if it smells like a duck, and it walks like a duck, and it quacks like a duck, then it's a duck."

Adjusting his chair a little closer to the table, "Guerra, you have to understand at this point and time you are a walk and one quack short of a duck."

"I appreciate what you are saying but what can I do to change your opinion?"

Taking a harder tone with the young soldier, "Nothing, you are a Grunt, an Infantryman and that's it. You are not trained in the investigative and legal field like we are." Agent M. Emmett said as he waved his thumb between him and his partner, Army CID Special Agent E. Walter.

Agent Ernest Walter for the first time spoke, "Have you told anyone else about this?"

"About what SSG Herndez did?"

"Yes"

"Just my roommates and they are the ones that told me to come to you."

"Can you trust them not to tell anyone?"

"Yes, I trust Wills, Ferriss, and Brown with my life," referring to the three soldiers, I shared a barracks room.

"Enough to bring you a cake with a hacksaw in it when you're locked up in the stockade for making false accusations?"

"Look, I know what I know and I know I can prove it!"

"How?"

"I don't know but I know I will."

If these guys don't start listening to me and start taking me seriously, I really feel that SSG Herndez is going to get away with murder. I know as soon as word gets back to him that I am here my life is going to become a living hell. Herndez is going to see to it. I know I would make life a living hell for anybody that accused me of murder. Heck, besides Herndez the rest of the US Army will make the rest of my time hell, all because I accuse one of their NCOs of killing a Private. The Army frowns upon those kinds of accusations. I know it is not the first time that someone accuses an NCO of murder and it will not be the last time but maybe, just maybe it is in my imagination and I am looking more into this than what it really is.

Imagination or not, I am way deep into this now. Here I am trying to make these CID agents believe something that they are trained to spot from the very beginning. I know I don't have the training, I certainly don't have the skills but I have my gut and my gut is telling me that Staff Sergeant Rafael Herndez is the man that is responsible for the death of my friend.

"Guerra!" snapping me out of my daydreaming and wishful thinking.

"Guerra! Do you have anything more to tell us?" asked CID Agent Walter.

"Just what I've been telling you all along, there is more to this than meets the eye. I know that on the surface, it looks like an accident but it is just too coincidental that Herndez randomly picked that spot for Vela to dig. No matter what you say about the Soviets and their trashing of Berlin, just what are the odds that he picked that right spot? You might say a million to one. I say a hole in one!"

"Do you understand the nature of what you're saying?" Walter asked.

"Yes, sir."

"Right now, there is nothing stopping me from charging you with making false statements to a CID agent, interfering with an investigation, slander, conduct unbecoming and anything else I can come up with. So do you still want to continue with this?" Walter asked with a little more authority.

"Yes, I understand and all I want is for somebody to listen to what I have to say and maybe think about where I'm coming from, see it from my point of view and maybe you might just find something. Even if it's just a little something I'll be happy and if then you want to charge me with something I'll take it."

"Tell you what. You are really passionate about this aren't you?" Emmett spoke after clearing his throat.

"Yes, sir. It's just the way I feel about the whole thing, the whole situation."

"This is what I am going to do. I should be doing some paper work but seeing as how you are really hung up about this, why don't you sit back and start from the beginning. Let's see what we can do to separate fact from fiction."

I said with a little relief in my voice, "Well, it began…"

CHAPTER THREE

WEST BERLIN • US SECTOR • McNAIR BARRACKS • BUILDING 1001B • A Co. 6th Battalion 502nd Infantry • SEPTEMBER 11, 1989 • MONDAY • 0430hrs

"ALERT! ALERT!" was coming from down the hall and doing the yelling was the Charge of Quarters NCO. The CQ almost immediately followed the call by two bangs on each door down the barracks hallway. Just like that, one of the buildings that housed members of the United States military presence in West Berlin was awake and buzzing with activity long before the sun even thought of rising over the Berlin Wall. Each soldier in the Berlin Brigade knew that when an Alert was activated they had a scant thirty minutes to get their weapon, helmet, rucksack, and duffel bag, and in some cases, live ammunition ready to hit the streets of West Berlin to fight the enemy and defend the citizens of West Berlin.

In 1989, that enemy was the Soviet Union, the East Germans, and the other member nations of the Warsaw Pact. It was also the year that the streaming of East Germans and other Eastern Europeans seemed to be a prelude to war. It was as if the Communists were throwing "refugees/defectors" across the Iron Curtain in an effort to throw West German and NATO forces off-balance by dealing with a humanitarian crisis. Then when the time was right, their tanks would roll through the Fulda Gap and leave Berlin alone by hanging a few *STALAG BERLIN* signs on the outside of the Berlin Wall.

Most certainly, the Cold War was still in full swing and the men and women of the Berlin Brigade found themselves 110 miles behind the front lines of that war, behind the Iron Curtain but in front of the Berlin Wall. It was because of this we practiced for the day that the Warsaw Pact decided to change the status quo.

9

"Come on Ferriss," I called over to my roommate, E-4 Percival Ferriss, "Get up fucker! You can't hide under those blankets forever!"

"Another Alert, another Monday morning. Want to guess where we're going?" Ferriss' voice came from deep within the pile of blankets.

"Doughboy, of course!" with a heavy dose of sarcasm I replied.

"You got it my friend, you got it. Das Doughboy City!"

Doughboy City is the Berlin Brigade's unofficial official name for a Military Operations in Urbanized Terrain training area located in the southwestern corner of Parks Range. Parks Range is located in the Lichterfelde district of the city of West Berlin. Doughboy City is a complex of concrete buildings arranged in a manner that simulated a small European town that allowed the members of the Army of Occupation of Berlin to train in a near realistic area that would involve kicking in doors, clearing rooms, and climbing stairwells. In West Berlin, kicking in real doors has not been allowed since the end of the Second World War.

Over the course of the next thirty minutes, the men of the Alpha Company, 6th Battalion, 502nd Infantry, as well as the rest of the men of the 6th Battalion's four other companies, start to get themselves ready for battle. This time, on this Alert, the battle is coming in the form of a road march, shooting blank ammunition and filling an almost endless supply of empty sandbags. Yet, that was part of being in a military unit that was ready to go to war in 30 minutes, you practice, practice, practice. So we go through the motions of getting ready to move out in the allotted thirty minutes.

As Ferriss and I moved our gear into the hallway, a line was starting to form by the Arms Room (weapons storage room) door. Fortunately, for us our room is located just across from the Arms Rooms so waiting to draw our weapon is never an issue. Being across the hall has its rewards, we can sit in our room, make and drink a pot of coffee before hitting the road.

I take a moment to look up and down the line filled with all the usual suspects. Each of my fellow soldiers stood patiently waiting for their turn to draw either an M16, an M16 with an M203 Grenade Launcher attached, an M60 Machine gun, or a 90MM Recoilless Rifle (which is more like an extra thick stove pipe than a rifle).

In that line are some soldiers that are more friends than associates and others that are more associates than friends. Nonetheless, we all came from the same place, the United States. All of us trained at the same basic training and advanced infantry-training base, Fort Benning, Georgia. We knew that if the ALERTS ever went from simulation to real world we were all we had. We would fight and, in most cases, die together. It was with that knowledge that an uneasy bond was forged that many before us and surely those after us would find that bond lasting a lifetime. While some of us knew each other better than others, we all knew that when the time came we had each other's back. No questions asked! No questions needed to be asked.

However, there were some individuals in Alpha Company that just gave off a bad vibe. Do not get me wrong, I know that when push came to shove they would be there. However, one of those that gave off such a bad vibe was at the end of the line but was quickly working his way up the line. He was an NCO (Non-Commissioned Officer), he was Staff Sergeant Rafael Herndez and just one look at him and you knew trouble was his middle name. It was not the overt kind of trouble that others can spot from a mile away, his was the kind of trouble that came from intimidating and all but terrorizing the lower ranked enlisted soldiers (E1 – E4). He would say and do things that would be just enough to get the job done but not enough to make any kind of charges stick. Of course, there were NCOs that were worse in the Army. However, being assigned to the Berlin Brigade was such an honor and it meant those with "problems" were not allowed in, so he had to have been groomed from within. Somewhere along the line, somebody taught Herndez that the life of an NCO meant forgetting that you were once a Private. Sure, the military discouraged fraternization but then again it also discouraged belittling subordinates and abusing power, of which this Staff Sergeant did often and sometimes without any regard of who may be watching or listening or both. In this case, having SSG Herndez assigned to A Company proved the adage that there is always, at least, one bad apple in the bunch. Luckily, he was assigned to second platoon and not to the third platoon that I was assigned. At least for now, he was somebody else's problem.

0500hrs…The time had come to move out.

SSG Mervyn Laffington, the Platoon Sergeant for 3rd Platoon, the platoon of 34 soldiers' most ranking NCO, called for everyone to move out and assemble outside. One by one the rooms started to empty as man, weapon, and gear moved in a clanking of metal, mesh, Kevlar, and boots all wrapped in camouflage to the assembly area outside and across the street from the barracks building.

"Damn! It's colder than a witch in a brass bra" Private Danny Driedl chirped as he walked out. For it being a mere ten days (or so) before the start of fall, the morning temperature was already hovering in the lower 40s.

"Hey Driedl, you going on Sick Call? 'cough' 'cough'" mockingly asked Specialist Sean Wils, a native of Connecticut but without the New England accent and attitude. He was one of the two M60 gunners for 3rd platoon. He was one of those guys that you knew had your back no matter what the situation and no matter who started it. We were good friends.

"Ha, ha, Fuck You! Specialist Wils." the five foot three, 18 year old with the pencil thin moustache by the name of Danny Driedl fired back and almost immediately recognized the error he had just made.

11

DAVID G. GUERRA

"Whoa! Looks like the Private is trying to grow a pair." Wils responded then added, "Private, you better chill out before I make you a permanent profile." Referring to the fact that Wils was not going to stand to be talked to like that by a Private (E-1) and that he was more disgusted at Driedl's inability to be a proper soldier because he had nasty habit of going on Sick Call when things started to get rough. This meant that everyone else in the platoon had to pick up Driedl's slack and do his job while he was out. While most of the other members of the Platoon were not OK with this but accepted his behavior, Wils was obviously getting tired of Driedl continually pulling one over on everyone. Making things even worse was that Driedl was the assistant M60 Gunner who had yet to carry the M60 on a road march or on an assault during the past six months since his arrival to the unit.

Approaching the loose gathering of men and equipment, SSG Laffington says, "Alright everyone, settle down, let's fall in."

"COMPANY FALL IN!" barked the Company First Sergeant, the unit's top NCO.

"Here it comes," Ferriss says to Guerra.

"At ease, back there!" Laffington says out of the side of his mouth to the two noisemakers in the formation behind him.

The Company Commander, Captain Daryl Bonds addressed us, "Alright Alpha Company, we are going to road march to Doughboy City and assault the city from the east at Sunrise it is now oh five oh five and Sunrise is just before Oh Seven Hundred. The Opposing Force moved into Doughboy last night and they are expecting a dawn attack. However, they were told to expect an attack from the South and West. You can rest assured we are going to catch them with their backside sticking out ready for us to kick."

"HOOOAH!" from throughout the company formation.

"Men, I promise you this if we can rout the OPFOR from the buildings we are going to attack, tonight we will sleep in our bunks but if we fail to take the objective we'll be right there all night until we take them out. So it behooves all of us to get it done right the first time."

Another round of "Hooahs" comes from within the formation.

"Alright men, let's get ready to go. First Sergeant get the company ready to move, let's line up in marching order."

"Company"

"Platoon"

"Fall out and fall in in marching order!"

Laffington barks, "Alright you heard the first sergeant we form up over here and we are on the left side of the road."

A few minutes later, two columns of soldiers, rucksacks, and weapons are marching out the front gate of McNair Barracks taking a left on Goerzallee, crossing the south entrance to Platz des 4 Juli (4th of July

12

Platz), then onto a cobble stone sidewalk until the next intersection. A right on busy Wismarer Strasse, then crossing over the famous Teltower Kanal. Straight on until the intersection with Ostpruessendamm where a left turn is taken. The column of a couple hundred men snakes through the sidewalks intermingling with a few pedestrians, parked cars, and even a couple of bicycles each trying to get an early start on the day. The journey did not take long but for anyone that ever road marched on cobble stone streets or sidewalks one thing was certain: you felt every one of those stones.

When the lead elements of the two columns reach the intersection with Osdorfer Strasse, the 6th Battalion of the 502nd Infantry Regiment made a right turn and straight on until we reached the front gate of Parks Range. It is at the gate where we stopped road marching and gather into company formation and prepare for the morning assault to the west with the rising sun at our backs.

"Alright Wils, you and Ferriss will flank each side with your 60s" Laffington started to get his platoon battle ready for the final assault.

"203 gunners you are to report to the CO location he's going to brief you on what they want you to do." The Platoon Sergeant continued, "Everyone else we are going to be on the right flank of the company and the company is the unit on the right side of the assault and you know what that means?"

"We're the FLANKING element!" someone among the predawn darkness responded.

"Buy that man a Berliner Kindl. Yes, we are going to wrap them up on the right side. So get ready to hoof it," SSG Laffington delivers the unwelcomed news.

"Damn, we're running again. Just our luck they laid concertina everywhere and we are going to dive head first into that crap." I was certainly not satisfied that we were the flanking element, again. However, I knew we would get the job done because we are just that good. I mean we are a great team because we take what we do seriously. We train hard, we play hard and when the time comes we will fight hard, that's just who we are. Better still, that is who we have become. But come on, you can use us but time and time again they keep lining us up like this, all I can think is please someone stop the abuse. I could complain but my mom is least 12,000 miles away and she did not vote for the Congressman that is currently in office. Oh well, maybe after the next election and that was still a year away. Besides, that does me no good now because it is time to get started.

We were off to fight today's battle.

CHAPTER FOUR

WEST BERLIN • US SECTOR • PARKS RANGE • DOUGHBOY CITY • AO ALPHA • SEPTEMBER 11, 1989 • 1037hrs

"Damn, I'm glad that's over," I said.

To finish things off we had to complete almost a 250-yard dash across an open muddy field carrying full combat gear before we could assault the last building of the day.

"Yeah, I nearly tripped over the concertina wire on that assault on the warehouse," Ferriss is referring to the barbed wire type material that was used as a way to slow down an enemy's advancement and deliberately direct them into an overlooking field of fire where a machinegun would take care of business.

"Damn! Look around! It looks like 4th Battalion used all the concertina they could find for this one."

A small framed lanky looking young soldier approaches the two, "Hey, Guys!"

"Vela, what's up?" Guerra recognizing PFC David Vela, a member of 2nd Platoon.

"The company is getting ready to form up. Looks like we are going to be doing something else."

"Come on, Guerra. Let's go, you know Mervyn will be looking for us."

"Here, help me up," I extended my hand only to have it ignored by Ferriss who turns and starts walking towards the company area.

"Alright, I see how that is. I'll remember that the next time you need someone to back you up…geez, this ruck is getting heavier and heavier," as I get up, throwing my rucksack over my head and onto my back.

"How's it going man, I haven't seen you since we ran into you and the missus on the Ku'damm?" I asked Vela as we headed over to the company area. Ferriss is just ahead but far enough away that he does not hear our conversation.

"Doing alright, just all this extra duty lately getting ready for this ARTEP."

"What extra duty?"

"Yeah, Herndez is always volunteering me for stuff and then when it is time to do it he is gone."

"Dang Dude, you should say something. That guy can't be doing shit like that to you."

"I tried talking to SFC Smithson and he said he would talk to Herndez"

"And?"

"…and nothing, that fucker gave me extra duty for having the platoon sergeant come down on him."

"Damn." I said in hush tone as we were getting close to the company area.

"Let's go! Fall in!" SSG Laffington called the platoon to fall in to formation.

Seconds later the company commander began talking to the men in formation in front of him, "Alright, first off let me start by saying good job. I knew that when the day started just six hours ago that we would complete our mission without problem. Alpha Company, you delivered and now I'm going to deliver. We are going in tonight!"

"HOOOAHHH!"

"Alright now before we can pack it in we have some work to do. We have to clean up this mess. Platoon Leaders and Platoon Sergeants you have your areas of responsibility so let's get started and we should be on the road no later than 1500 hours, ok let's get started, fall out!"

"Alright third platoon, we have the area that covers the warehouse, Guerra and Ferriss seeing as how you two already know the area take weapons squad over to the field between that house and the warehouse and collect the concertina and stack it next to the building."

The other M60 Machine Gunner, two Assistant Gunners, two 90mm Recoilless Rifle gunners, and the two assistant gunners move back to where Guerra and Ferriss were when Vela first called on them to go to formation.

They begin to collect the almost never-ending strands of concertina wire.

"Hey Guerra, did you really run into Vela and his wife on the Ku'damm?"

"Yeah, it was a couple of Saturdays ago, Ann and I saw them coming out the Europa Center as we were going in."

"Man, Vela's wife is smoking hot."

"Oh yeah she's a looker. I look at her and look at him and think what does she see in him?"

"He must have a big schwanz. That has to be the only reason that she is with him. They just don't add up, if you know what I mean?"

"Yeah, that's why Ann is with me. You know…my big schwanz."

"Man, shut the fuck up and toss me that wire," Ferriss says as I toss over a re-bundled strand of concertina wire.

SEPTEMBER 11, 1989 • 1404hrs

"Damn it! Son of a Bitch!" Vela says aloud as he walks over to Guerra and Ferriss to pass along the latest.

"Oh Crap, what good news do you bring us now Vela?"

"Staff Sergeant Herndez volunteered me for guard duty tonight."

"Man, that guy has it in for you big time."

"Yeah, what did you do to piss him off?" asked Ferriss.

"I don't know, we like him and he's pretty cool when we are off-duty. So I don't know, anyway every platoon has to leave behind somebody to help guard all the barricade gear until the Engineers come pick it up in the morning."

Looking at each other both Guerra and Farrell yell, "COVENTRY!"

"Don't sweat it Vela, it ain't nothing but a thing." Ferriss tells Vela in a sympathetic tone. As Ferriss knows all too well, what it is like to be picked on by the higher-ranking NCOs. When he first arrived, Laffington zeroed right in on Ferriss and made life Hell for him. Then when I arrived the heat was off of him but now on me. That lasted all of a couple of weeks when Private James Coventry arrived in the city and Laffington found someone new to treat like crap by giving him all the crap assignments.

However, both Ferriss and I wondered, "Why Vela?" and why for so long, other rag-bag goof-offs were assigned to 2nd Platoon long after Vela's arrival. Yet, the crappy details were still being given to Vela.

"Yeah, I know and I understand that's the price I pay for being a Private but come on, not even Tyler gets volunteered this much," Vela was referring to another member of 2nd platoon that was the one that was getting volunteered the most before he arrived to Alpha Company.

"Tyler told me one day, he wishes that he was still getting picked on, if only to help take some of the heat off of me. He also told me that he wanted to volunteer for something and that Herndez told him to stand down or he would write him up and recommend an Article 15 for failure to comply and failure to follow a direct order and something else."

"Well, think about this. Tonight will be fire barrel time. If we get back in time and depending on who is on staff duty tonight we'll hook you up with some pogey bait," I was referring to some goodies such as candies, chocolates, sodas, and various sundries that would make this BS detail bearable. If one of us knew the Staff Duty Officer, Staff Duty NCO, or Staff Duty Runner we could accompany them or just throw in a bag of goodies in the back of the Humvee when they made their rounds to Doughboy.

It was around 1600 hours that the company finally started moving back to McNair Barracks at the corner of Goerzallee and Platz des 4.Juli. McNair was always a welcome sight no matter if we were at Doughboy for a week, a 12 mile DBC Road March or spending a month in the zone (West Germany) at Wildflecken, Hammelburg or at some other Truppenubungsplatz. It was home for the single soldiers, it was where we slept, ate, trained, and worked. Yet, with its Burger Bar, Movie Theater, Bank, Small PX, Rod and Gun Club, Book Store, Barber Shop, Tailor Shop, Laundromat, it was not home but it certainly helped make the time tolerable, especially for those that missed home. With all these amenities, I could only imagine what life was like for the soldiers of the 1960s, -50s, and late -40s when things were still fresh with the occupation of Berlin. Then again, one thing I know for sure, the soldiers that were in Berlin during the Blockade and the Berlin Airlift would definitely call us spoiled and soft.

Then again, those were different times. Their hard work and sacrifice has helped keep the peace for over 40 years and trust me, it is very much appreciated. By the time I landed at Tegel Airport, the Berlin I was experiencing had already undergone though growing pains. Those pains came from the recovering from ashes of the fallen Nazi capital to the division of the city by a scar that stood 13 feet tall and ran right down the middle of it to becoming the shining example of Capitalism in a sea of Communism.

"COMPANY FALLOUT!" snapping out of my daydream.

Making my way into the company area, I ask the CQ (Charge of Quarters NCO), "Sergeant Madagh, who is the Staff Duty NCO tonight?"

"SSG Lancaster from CSC"

"Thanks."

A phone call, a little negotiating, some finagling, and one favor later Vela, Coventry, and the rest of the guys on guard duty were going to get some top level pogey bait. Normally, when we know we are going to be out there for more than a day we pack accordingly. However, today was an exception so we were all caught a little short.

I had to hurry and get this done if I wanted to see Ann tonight. It had to be an early night as she had her first Literature test of the semester tomorrow. Yet, with Ferris' help, somehow I managed to get the pogey bait and myself out the front gate within an hour after turning in our weapons. It was 1840 hours.

CHAPTER FIVE

WEST BERLIN • US SECTOR • McNAIR BARRACKS • A COMPANY, 6th BATTALION, 502nd INFANTRY • 3rd PLATOON DAYROOM • SEPTEMBER 22, 1989 • FRIDAY • 0900HRS

"Alright, Third Platoon listen up..." SSG Mervyn Laffington, the pride of East Texas, says as he briefs the platoon on the next week's activities and today's before the end of the day activities. Obviously, the platoon members are ready for the weekend to begin. However, there was work to be done first.

"Wils, you, Ferris, Guerra, and Brown at thirteen hundred hours will link up with the First Sergeant for a trip to Doughboy City."

"Sergeant Laffington, can't you send Covington and the other Privates?" asked Wils.

"I am sending you! One more thing out of any of you four and you will find yourselves in the front leaning rest position for the whole weekend and no goofing around at Doughboy."

The front leaning rest position was the Army term for the position to assume before doing Push-ups. Push-ups! So far, during my brief time in the Army I have done so many push-ups that the Earth's axis has probably shifted about a degree to the right. Then again, what's a few more? However, something else I learned in that time; less push-ups is better.

"Yes, Sergeant Laffington."

"Covington, Driedl, Vance, and Schotze will report to the Mess Hall Parking Lot, you will be helping to pack the Field Kitchen."

Moaning and groaning came from the back of the room. As anyone that has ever worked with the Mess Hall Staff knows, 'helping' means doing all the work for the cooks. It also means opening the already sealed Field

18

Kitchen, taking everything out, testing the burners, cleaning everything, packing the kitchen, and then sealing it shut. That usually takes about six hours on a good day. However seeing, as it is Friday, a new record time was going to be set.

"Alright you four, move out, Schotze you are the ranking Private," and with that the four lowest ranking privates in the platoon move out to attend to their assignment for the day.

The rest of the meeting was more aimed at the NCOs of 3rd Platoon to ensure that all the personal gear was ready. Ensuring everyone understood that while it was not an "official" announcement of an "alert" for Monday morning it was the start of another Red Block week and that meant another week of training at Doughboy City.

It also meant going through the Monday Morning Hell that begins with the CQ banging on all the doors down the company hallways and initiating the Alert. Then it is 100 miles per hour until after the first objective is met, which is either an assault on a force that is already in place or setting up defensive positions and waiting for the inevitable assault from the Opposing Force (OPFOR).

McNAIR BARRACKS • COMPANY A, 6th BATTALION, 502nd INFANTRY • COMPANY AREA • SEPTEMBER 22, 1989 • FRIDAY • 1300HRS

"OK, men I asked for all the 60 and 90 gunners and their assistants to meet me here. We are going to load up on the Deuce and a half and go to Doughboy City and look at fighting positions for next week. Any questions?"

"No, First Sergeant!"

"Alright then get in the back of the deuce and half and let's go" referring to the US Army's M35 2 ½ ton weight class truck that is part of the US Armed Forces wheeled motor vehicle pool. It is typically used to move men, supplies, and equipment from a rear logistical center to the front lines with minimum concern on terrain as the vehicle is raised considerably off the ground and has a wide wheelbase that it can climb steep angles with minimal effort. It was the Army's workhorse and that is because it was designed to be a workhorse.

Once on board I spot Vela and Tyler already on board and sit by them.

"Hey men, wie gehts?"

"Wondering if we are going to have to start filling sandbags?"

"Yeah, another scheisse detail," Tyler says as the truck starts driving down towards the main gate and onto Goerzallee, rounding the bend past Parkfriedhof Lichterfelde, crossing the Teltower Canal and onwards to Doughboy.

The deuce and a half truck is equipped with a very loud 170 Horse Power Caterpillar Diesel Engine so any form of communication has to be at an elevated level. For the major part of the ride the conversation is almost non-existent.

Once the vehicle turns onto Parks Range, the attitude of the men on board the back of the M35 Truck returns to that of wondering what is really going on. The vehicle continues to the back of the range to a wooded area that is used as a staging area for the opposing forces. The wooded area provides excellent cover and concealment for the attacking force as they can begin the assault on the defending forces from any one of three sides and is only made known when the force crests the hill in front of Doughboy City. However, there was a clearing further west and to the south of this wooded area, no one usually attacked from that side.

The area beyond the clearing was actually East Germany. At this point in the geographic layout of West Berlin, the city limits butt right up against the East German state of Brandenburg. While the division between East Berlin and West Berlin is the notorious "Berlin Wall", the division between West Berlin and East Germany is a wall at some points but a tightly wound mesh fence here and other "strategic" locations along the rest of the border. No matter where the wall or the fence are, on the East side, there are always roads for vehicles to drive on, tank traps, dog runs, electronic trigger alarm systems, and guard towers with their binoculars, cameras, and plenty of live ammunition.

This spot, where the US forces trained and the East German border met, was no exception as there was a tower usually manned by two Border Guards and mounted patrol are always driving. However, when any of the Allies start their exercises at Doughboy City the vehicle traffic on the East German side of the fence picks up and rivals any major rush hour traffic jam. The East Germans and Soviets gather to witness our time on the mock battlefield.

The truck finally comes to a stop and everyone dismounts. The company first sergeant explains the situation and within 15 minutes, each Gunner/Assistant Gunner Team is walking around to find where their hasty fighting position will be. As they will be providing covering fire to the assaulting force. They will all be on top of the hill shooting down while the attack is underway. The plan is to keep the defender's heads down until it is too late and the attackers start knocking on the doors of the mock city.

One gunner asks the First Sergeant if we will be filling sandbags as a hasty fighting position does not always mean digging armpit deep or overhead cover. The First Sergeant tells everyone, "We plan on getting here early enough to put a front and side of sand bags two deep before the assault begins. That's why we are here now to see where everyone goes and not try to figure it out at the last minute at Oh Dark Thirty under light and noise discipline."

"Hooaah, First Sergeant!"

"Alright, finish finding your spots and let's get it marked so you know. We won't have time for anyone to mess up so let's get it right."

About 30 minutes later they all start walking back to get on the truck for the trip back. I met up with Vela, "Hey, what's up? You been looking a little beat."

"Nothing just wife problems, you wouldn't understand."

"Wouldn't understand? I will have you know I am a product of a broken home, you ain't seen problems like I have seen problems."

"This is different, so very different."

"The two of you going downtown tonight?"

"If I can avoid Herndez when we get back."

"Man, is he still giving you trouble?"

"Yeah, after the guard duty he has been real angry and really busting my ass every chance he gets. Now, I dread looking at him every day," catching his breath Vela continues, "Do you know what he did while I was on Guard Duty?"

"I don't know."

"At around 1 in the morning, he comes driving up with the Staff Duty NCO to check on us."

"Did he say anything to you?"

"No, the Staff Duty NCO asked us questions, he just sat there and stared at me the whole time. I think I answered the questions right. But then after, in the morning, when I got back to the barracks I was putting my gear in my wall locker and he asked me where I was going and I told him that I was going home. Then he got real quiet and walked out of the room and I went home."

"Hmmm," I said.

"Why did you ask?"

"Just trying to figure out why he is picking on you. Then again, he must really like you because Laffington wouldn't come out at one o'clock in the morning. Mervyn doesn't give a damn about us unless one of two things is happening. Either we make him look good or we make him look bad then and only then does he care."

We make it back to where the truck is parked. As I hop on the back of the truck, I look at Vela and for a brief moment, it looked like he was crying. That thought quickly left me as the vehicle lurched when it was turned on and that made everyone reach for a strap or something to hold on to in order to avoid falling on top of anyone or out the back of the vehicle. The vehicle was off and we were on our way back to McNair.

21

McNAIR BARRACKS • COMPANY A, 6th BATTALION, 502nd INFANTRY • COMPANY AREA • SEPTEMBER 22, 1989 • FRIDAY • 1525HRS

"Alright, remember what we talked about on the hill. You are the best at what you do and that's why I took you today so that we could be just one-step ahead of the 4th Battalion. I wanted you to have an idea of what the situation will be like when we hit the ground Monday morning. OK go back to your Platoon Sergeants and tell them that I have released you for the day. For those of you in First and Second Platoons, as you make your way back to your Area of Operations (AO) I better not hear that you made fun of, laughed at, or gave a hard time to the people working on the Field Kitchen or you will find yourself working right next to them for the next three months. Is that understood?"

"Yes, First Sergeant."

"OK, Dismissed!"

"HOO FREAKING AAAHHHH!"

The weekend has begun for, at least, some of the soldiers of Alpha Company 6th Battalion, 502nd Infantry Regiment, the others were dismissed just after lunch to include the majority of the NCOs. Herndez was one of them and was now nowhere to be seen in the barracks. This was not a big surprise as that was usually the case when time off was given, no one that was off stayed in the immediate area for any extended period of time for fear of being called in to perform some duty or lead a detail like raking snow around the company area. It was somewhat difficult to find someone to do something when no one was around. Slowly but surely, the members of Alpha Company started to trickle out into the late fall afternoon and onto the streets of the only occupied city in the world: West Berlin.

CHAPTER SIX

WEST BERLIN • US SECTOR • PARKS RANGE • DOUGHBOY CITY • PHASELINE GOLD • SEPTEMBER 25, 1989 • MONDAY • 0745HRS

Again, the unit was brought to life by the banging on the room doors, the yelling and the thirty-minute time limit. However, this time the call did not come in at 0430 hours. It came an hour earlier and by 0415, the unit was well on its way back to the concrete city to keep our Combat in the Cities skills sharp and ready for when they were actually needed. This morning, we were looking forward to trying something different when we assaulted the city. However, just as dawn was beginning to break a fog rolled across East and West Berlin.

This fog quickly grew thick, so thick that it would be the normal "sometime tomorrow" before signs of burning off would start to show. The commanding officer decided to take advantage of the situation and give the men on top of the hill a longer opportunity to fortify their hasty fight positions. The extra time gave the assaulting force an opportunity to grab a quick meal before the sun rose higher and forced the assault.

We could not see any further than five or six feet in any direction, I said to myself, "It's like the First Sergeant has ESP making sure that we knew where our positions were."

Ferriss looks at , "Did you say something?" thinking he heard something.

"No, I was just thinking about 1SG Kiddle and how adamant he was that we knew where our positions should be today of all days."

"Yeah."

"It's like he just knew that the fog was gonna roll in."

"You know if we were back in Oklahoma."

"Oh, here we go."

"Seriously, he would be one that had a high status in the tribe. Because he would be considered one of those people that can tell you when bad or good things were coming."

"Yeah, but Kiddle did not stand there and do a fog dance, he just said for us to make sure we knew where we were going to be."

"They don't flat out tell you it is going to rain at this time or it will snow but they can just feel it."

"OK gotcha, that's it…he just felt it."

"And that's why he has high status in the unit."

"Yeah I guess that's why he's the First Sergeant. Anyway, are you going to fire up a heat tab 'cause I want some hot coffee?"

"Are we done with the sand bags?"

"Yeah I think so, I left two half-filled bags back there," pointing back to where I was filling the sandbags to complete the front and sides of the fighting position, "just in case Laffington decides to show up and tell us what we're doing wrong again."

"Good, hopefully he'll stay in the CP until just before they decide to attack."

"This should be interesting seeing them attack from up here or at least hear it," referring to the thick fog blanketing the battlefield.

"It will be nice to not be lugging this beast down that hill then up and down the streets of Doughboy."

"Careful what you say, they could at the last minute tell us to follow them on the attack."

All up and down the line of 90MM Recoilless Rifles and M60 Machineguns the men of Alpha Company are settling themselves in for a quick rest before chaos breaks the morning calm and the flashes and bangs change the tone of the day. Before the line of men and weapons of war, the ground will shake and the sky will fill with artificial clouds. The smoke of burning tires, smoke grenades, and wood will hang close to the ground replacing the grey and white of the morning fog.

What seems like an hour is only a few minutes later that the word comes down for everyone to put another layer of bags in place. More digging, more bags.

"Alright, be right back," as I move out to get started on filling and moving sand bags.

As I started filling the two half-empty bags I could hear some discussion just off to the right and on the other side of the fog. I recognized the voices.

"Vela, move down to the edge of the tree line there and dig there."

"Staff Sergeant Herndez, I've already started here and the soil is loose I don't mind hauling the bags down to the position"

"Vela, move over there now, that is a direct order private."

"Yes, Sergeant."

The sounds of the two fade away and I could no longer hear the Private and the NCO. I was starting to think to myself, "yeah that's all I need for Laffington to tell me to move closer to the position and start digging from scratch."

WEST BERLIN, GERMANY • PARKS RANGE • WOODED STAGING AREA • SEPTEMBER 25, 1989 • MONDAY • 0805HRS

I had just finished filling and delivering about eight sandbags when suddenly and violently the morning erupts with a blast that sounds like hell opened up and took everything in its path back into the seven levels with it. It was so bright that the fog cloud lit up like one of the those East German Tower spotlights shining right in your eyes when you get too close to the wall; blinding and engulfing.

A horrific howl was mixed with the sound of the blast and the arresting light. I was certain it was a howl. Then the ringing in my ears began.

Along with the noise, the concussion wave was strong enough to move the fog out of the way and knock down the sand bags off the stack that made the front and sides of just about all the hasty fighting positions along the front line.

The first thing I thought was that the force in the mock city had given up waiting and decided to attack instead of defending. Then I could hear faint popping sounds, over the ringing in my ears. I could tell that it was not close and I saw no one over running our position. It was obvious the defending forces at Doughboy City thought that they were being attacked, as well. Yet, over the noise and ringing, I knew something was not right.

I reached over the bags to see if Ferriss was all right. "Percy, you ok?" shaking his shoulder I found him unresponsive. "Ferriss! Are you ok?"

Just then, Ferriss picks his head up, "What was that?"

Something was definitely not right with this picture. I saw Ferriss about three feet over from where his shoulder is or was it his shoulder? I saw a camouflage pattern BDU top, a hand. I felt a shoulder but then as I looked over the top of the sandbags I saw part of a torso and nothing more, nada, nichts.

Immediately, throughout the front line the word "MEDIC!" is heard over the popping noises and grenade simulators going off down in Doughboy city.

"Holy Shit!!! What the hell is that, I mean who the hell is this? What happened?" Ferriss and I started to see for ourselves that this was once part of somebody in a US Army Battle Dress Uniform top with part of somebody still in it.

"Where is the rest of him? MEDIC! Sergeant Laffington! MEDIC!"

"What happened? The East Germans the Russians are they attacking?"

"No, it wasn't the Soviets or the East Germans," Laffington said as he approached the two, "There would be more than just one round. Whoa, shit what the hell is that?" almost swallowing the tobacco dip he had just inside his front lower lip.

"I thought it was Ferriss but here he is, all of him."

"Are you two OK?"

"Yes."

"Who is over there?"

"That's where 2nd Platoon starts...oh shit it's..."

"You two stay here let me go see and put a poncho over that," pointing to the arm.

In the background the calls for a medic continue. Down in Doughboy City intermixed with the grenade simulators, M16 and M60 blank rounds are calls to 'Cease Fire'! Slowly, an uneasy quiet starts to return across Doughboy City except for noise of confused people and name-calling and questions, many questions.

Through the fog, I was starting to make out Laffington's voice as the ringing in my ears was fading when I could clearly hear him say, "The rest is over there by Guerra and Ferriss' position." Then it got quiet again.

"Who do you think it is?" asked Ferris.

"I don't know but damn this is worse than when Sgt. Stracklind let the artillery simulator go off in his hand."

"Yeah, this is way worse than that. Have you ever seen anything like this?"

"No, but from the sounds of the medic calls there are others that are seeing parts of him too"

Just then, the company First Sergeant walks up and asks, "You two ok?"

"Yes, First Sergeant."

"Where is he?"

"Under the poncho"

The Company First Sergeant bends down to pick up the poncho, looks underneath and says, "we have to find his head."

"Damn, his head is missing?" I ask in disbelief.

"It's probably down there," pointing down the hill towards Doughboy.

Ferriss without missing a beat says, "You want us to go look for it, First Sergeant?"

"No, you two stay here. Don't go anywhere, guard this, and wait for the Medics and when the MPs get here they are going to want to talk to you," and as if on cue sirens are heard off in the distance getting louder. They are definitely getting louder and closer.

"Uh First Sergeant, who is it?" Ferriss asking the question.

"We are not sure we are getting a head count. Someone from 2nd Platoon it looks like," the First Sergeant says as he turns to leave to the next position to get people started on finding the missing head and anything else that may be missing.

"Oh Shit!" names started popping in my head. I was able to remove from the list of possibilities because of skin color, others I was not too sure about, there were just too many to imagine.

A few minutes later, a voice just beyond the fog yells, "We found Vela's head!"

"Mother…fuck, it was Vela. Son of a bitch went and got himself killed," those were the first words that came out of my mouth as the second shock of the morning started setting in.

"Damn it! What the fuck was that explosion? I mean it tore him apart," asked Ferriss.

"I don't know. It was huge. Did you see the shirt? It had a lot of little tears like shrapnel but that was too loud for a hand grenade."

WEST BERLIN, GERMANY • PARKS RANGE • WOODED STAGING AREA • ALPHA COMPANY AREA • SEPTEMBER 25, 1989 • MONDAY • 1130HRS

The fog was lifting and we were starting to see the war zone and the crater at the epicenter. It was a miracle that there were no more injuries other than light shrapnel wounds along with some hearing issues. Training was canceled but no one on the hill was to leave until things were sorted. The remains of Private David Vela were collected and transported to the 279th Station Hospital for the first stage of processing him for the long trip home. Now the investigation begins.

The investigators of the 287th Military Police Company, Army Criminal Investigation Division (CID), Army EOD, Berlin Polizei, Feuerwehr, and other assorted agents of the US Intelligence Community were on the scene talking to everyone, trying to make sense of what happened and how. Of course, on the other side of the fence is a large contingent of Soviet and East German military vehicles, troops (officer and enlisted), and cameras, both still and motion picture. At this point, they are just a few tanks and helicopters short of an invasion but that is subject to change at almost any minute, as this part of the district of Lichterfelde was quickly becoming the center of Berlin.

As the area was cordoned off, the scar on the ground was plainly visible. Whatever it was that went off certainly made a big dent on the earth.

"Mortar Rounds, either right on top or just under the surface," the Army EOD officer told the Alpha Company Commander.

The Lead CID Investigator asked, "Are you sure?"

"You know that this part of Berlin has plenty of unexploded Soviet 50 millimeter Mortar rounds," the EOD officer continued, "as the Battle for Berlin raged, near the end of the World War II, the Soviet Union amassed so many men, so much equipment that the amount of bullets, mortars and bombs that were shot at or landed within the city limits was more than the total tonnage of bombs dropped from Allied airplanes over the City of Berlin during the entire war. Many of the bombs, rockets, and mortars were either just left behind or landed unexploded. No matter what and no matter how long ago they are very much live ammo. As the years have gone by these munitions become more and more unstable that something as simple as an acorn falling from an Oak tree and landing on top of one of them would set it off."

"The squad leader said he made Private Vela move to that area so that he would be closer to the unit because of the dense fog. It seems that he dug in the one spot that had at least three 50-millimeter mortar rounds. The shovel, which we haven't found, must have hit one which set off the other two either laying real close or underneath," the Investigator concluded.

"So this was just a terrible accident?"

"Looks like it."

"When was the last time EOD came out and did a sweep?"

"We don't usually sweep here, we sweep where the troops bivouac or mount and dismount vehicles and as far as I know no one has ever made any type of hasty fighting position let alone fill any sandbags up here. We sweep Doughboy City at least once a month to make sure that our friends across the fence there haven't dropped something unexpected, that way no one gets a nasty surprise."

"Has the wife been notified?" asked the Company Commander.

"They are doing that now the Brigade Chaplain, Red Cross Representative, and a Casualty Officer."

"Damn, what a waste."

"Yes, it is. They always are especially with these kinds of accidents. Essentially, he is the latest casualty of the Second World War. Oh, I have been asked to remind you to remind your men about the media. AFN Berlin is already getting calls from all the major news sources in the States and in Berlin. The CG (Commanding General) does not want this to become an international incident."

"Too late, we're in Berlin someone serves you ketchup instead of mayo with your pommes frites it's an international incident. When can I get my men back to McNair?"

"I think we have a few things left to do, you can start clearing the AO with the exception of the marked off areas. The men that discovered the parts we have just a couple of questions to ask them other than that it should be no more than another 30 or 40 minutes. If you want, we can radio in to have some buses brought in to take everyone in? They are staged at the Four Ring."

"Yes, please," turning towards the First Sergeant, "First Sergeant, will you get the company formed up at the base of the hill and have everyone that discovered the parts form up by the tape over there."

The First Sergeant moved to the bottom of the hill that lead to Doughboy City and called the company to fall in. Once we were in formation, he called Ferriss, myself, and the other soldiers that the Investigators needed to speak to, again. Before loading onto the buses the company First Sergeant proceeded to explain what happened and what was going to happen especially when it came to talking to others outside of the unit about what happened.

The buses were starting to pull up for that ride home. It would turn out to be our longest ride ever because this time we were going back one man short.

CHAPTER SEVEN

WEST BERLIN, GERMANY • US SECTOR • US ARMY TRANSPORTATION BRANCH PASSENGER BUS • TRAVELING TO McNAIR BARRACKS FROM PARKS RANGE • SEPTEMBER 25, 1989 • MONDAY • 1330HRS

Sitting there on the bus it was quiet. So quiet you could hear the Mercedes diesel engine and every cobblestone on the road the tires drove over the entire ride back to McNair. I got to thinking. I was replaying the entire morning from the road march to everything. Something just was not right and I was thinking about the conversation Herndez and Vela had. Then it hit me, something happened last month just after the start of the German-American Volksfest there was an incident on the 10 bus back to McNair...

WEST BERLIN, GERMANY • US SECTOR • BVG #10 BUS • TRAVELING FROM BVG OSKAR-HELENE-HEIM BAHNHOF TO McNAIR BARRACKS • AUGUST 6, 1989 • SUNDAY • 2245HRS

"You little shit!"

"Excuse me Sergeant," obviously surprised and confused I responded.

"You think you are the shit, don't you?"

"I'm sorry Sergeant, I don't know what you are talking about."

"You damn well know what I am talking about Private" the smell of whiskey was strong on Staff Sergeant Herndez, obviously from a night at the NCO Club, across the street from Oskar-Helene-Heim, which was more than enough for the E-6. It had to be the NCO Club because the hardest stuff they sold at the Volksfest was Michelob beer. Those Berliners really liked our beer. Then again we really liked (and still do) their Berliner Kindl.

"Sergeant, you need some rest, you look really, really tired," I was trying not to tell him the obvious.

"Tell you what Private, we'll go back to your place and I will get some of that good rest again...ha ha ha," as he puts his head down on the seat back of the chair in front of him.

He called me Private two times. The last time I was a Private was three months ago. Yeah, that was a promotion that Laffington did not like one bit. He flat out told me that I was not to put on the E-4 rank because as far as he was concerned I did not deserve it. One thing is certain, I did not ask for the promotion but I got it. My Leave and Earnings Statement had it in writing, E-4 as my assigned rank. There was no denying it, if the person who signs my check says I have been promoted then guess what? I have been promoted.

Anyway, who and what was Herndez talking about.

As the Berlin BVG number 10 bus pulls to the stop in front of McNair Barracks, I contemplated waking Herndez up or not and letting him take the ride to the end of the route. If he remembers whom he was really talking to there would be hell to pay then again if he still thinks he was talking to a Private, then that Private had hell to pay for no particular reason. Serves the Privates right, I remember having to pay my dues coming up the ranks, so why not pass along a little hell to the young Privates? Let there be hell to pay and with that, I turned and walked out the door after the bus came to a complete stop.

Walking up to the Gatehouse worked by members of the 6941st Guard Battalion, I showed my US Army Identification card to the young Berliner that works as a part of the Local National Guard Force. The members of the 6941st were a force composed of local citizens that worked various jobs in support of the mission of the US Army and US Air Force in Berlin. The tasks that they performed ran the gamut of base security, to assisting with traffic control, to firing range access control, and even as technical and liaison assistants when the situation called for it. These men and women had a thankless job especially when it came to dealing with drunk GI's on any given night in Berlin. Yet, they remained professional no matter the situation or the job they were performing.

WEST BERLIN, GERMANY • US SECTOR • McNAIR BARRACKS • McNAIR CHAPEL • SEPTEMBER 28, 1989 • THURSDAY • 1130HRS

The memorial service for Private First Class David Vela (posthumously promoted) had just ended and everyone was walking back to the company area, which was just across the street. The entire ceremony was very quiet, somber, and had the military pomp and circumstance mixed in, to include the 21-gun salute, and a bugler from the 298th Army Band played Taps. At the end, a Bagpiper from the British Military Band played Amazing Grace. There were members of the French Forces, the Berlin Polizei, the press, and family members of those from Alpha Company. For many of the people there it was their first time attending such an event as it was far from the typical civilian ceremony. It made it memorable in that not only was this someone everyone worked and lived with, Vela was someone they knew.

The eulogies were touching and to the point. Friends and Leaders spoke about the man, the soldier, the friend. When Vela's wife came up to the podium, she dropped a bomb of her own. It was also the saddest part of the entire ceremony when Vela's wife announced to everyone that she was pregnant. The room went even more silent. It was at that moment that many of the married soldiers and their spouses in the chapel realized one of their worst fears was becoming a reality, a soldier will not be around to see their child be born, grow up, and have children of their own.

It was also at this moment that something inside of me told me that what Vela's wife was saying was more of a declaration than an announcement because she was looking at one individual in the front of the chapel when she said what she said.

It was not until the receiving line that I spotted something that set off an alarm in my head. When everyone went past Vela's wife, they either shook her hand or gave her a hug, which she appeared to genuinely accept. That is until it was Herndez' turn, when he reached over to hug her, she was already pushing him away. She tried to cover up the look of disgust that was slowly creeping onto her face and almost did a good job. However, some still came through and when I looked at her, I saw it plain as day. Something was definitely not right with the picture and I just could not place it. Something about those three was more than meets the eye and now with Vela gone there was something bigger going on that I could not fully grasp, at least not yet.

Once my roommates and I were back in the barracks room, we got out of our Class A's and into civilian clothes. We were done for the day. Nothing more was planned at least until 0600 tomorrow morning with PT, then spending the rest of the day talking to the investigators again as they were still not done with those that were there. Having been asked the same questions over and over again Ferriss and I were starting to wonder why did Vela's left arm have to land right in the middle of our hasty fighting position? Then again, the bigger question we kept asking ourselves is why did Vela have to die?

Wils breaks the silence, "I don't care what anyone says that was still some fucked up shit!"

"What was?" Brown responds a little confused about Wils' comment.

"How this guy has this smoking hot wife, a baby on the way, and then he just gets blown up like that?"

"That's the great 'U s qu a ni go di'," Ferriss replied.

"Huh?" I had never heard Ferriss say that word, I had heard other Cherokee words but not that one.

"Usqu a ni go di is mystery in Cherokee. That which is unknown or uncertain. That's just the way things are and we will never know why they happen, they just do."

"See and that's what is so screwed up about it, we will never know," Wils answers back.

"And I see your frustration, because it is like some Russian soldier from forty years ago was in so much of hurry that he left a couple of mortar rounds behind in a wooded area only to be found in 1989 by an American Soldier that was digging in the ground to fill a fucking sand bag."

"Yeah, and now he gets the big plane ride to the states."

"What time did the First Sergeant say the plane was going to take off?" It was nice of the Air Force people at Tempelhof to do a flyover with the plane carrying Vela over the barracks one last time. Forty minutes later the C-141 aircraft carrying the remains of PFC Vela, his pregnant widow and all their household goods were on their way home after flying a little lower than expected. Everyone on the grounds of McNair Barracks stopped looked up and saluted.

CHAPTER EIGHT

WEST BERLIN, GERMANY • US SECTOR • McNAIR BARRACKS • 6th BATTALION, 502nd INFANTRY BATTALION • DINING FACILITY • OCTOBER 2, 1989 • MONDAY • 0730HRS

I was in line with Ferriss, Wils, and Brown for breakfast. The Dining Facility is located in the basement of the 6th Battalion barracks. It unfortunately is the only facility for the five Infantry companies that comprise the 6th Battalion, 502nd Infantry Regiment. The chow line, as it is known, moves pretty fast when the meal options are limited. It was not a four-star restaurant, however, it was the only place serving an American style breakfast in this part of the city. For a Friday morning, the line was not as long as it is most other mornings.

As we grabbed our trays full of breakfast and coffee, we made our way towards our usual table along the back wall. Here we settle in for a nice leisurely meal that we normally do not finish until moments before the 9 o'clock formation.

"Hey, Guerra!"

"Hey, Wils?"

"You remember back in Wildflecken when we ate with the Bundeswehr at breakfast?"

The Wildflecken Training Area is a military base in West Germany where US, German, and NATO member nations would send their forces to conduct live fire exercises on any of the numerous firing ranges on the complex. It was not uncommon to have forces from several nations on the facility grounds at any given time. While in Berlin, there were firing ranges for the various weapon systems the US Forces kept in its arsenal, there was one exception. Due to quadpartitie agreements, the firing of live machinegun ammunition was prohibited. Therefore, Wildflecken was one of a handful of bases in West Germany that were equipped and had the space to handle machinegun live fire. So once or twice a year, depending on the need or mission, one battalion at a time would rotate out of the city and travel by the US Duty Train through East Germany and wake up just as the train would pull in to the Wildflecken Bahnhof.

"Yeah, why?"

"Who was that guy that sat across from you? It was as if you two had known each other."

"Oh yeah, that was Allred. We were in Basic Training together. Yeah, he was the last person I expected to see in Wildflecken," I answered, "Why do you ask?"

"That was one tall goofy looking mother..." Wils' true nature of the conversation came out.

I chuckled, "Well he's a good guy and the kind you know has your back in a fight. Besides it was good to see an old familiar face."

"Well, that was a face."

"Anyway, I wonder what CID is going to want us to do today?" I asked.

"More of the same...what we saw and what we heard."

"Yeah, we all saw the same thing nothing but fog," Brown chimed in.

"I will never forget the sounds," Ferriss adding to the conversation.

"Yeah, I could have sworn I heard him, like howl out loud mixed in with the explosion." I finally said it.

"Damn, I thought I was the only one," Wils answered back.

"It had to be him, it was deep and hallow," Ferriss said.

Brown summed it all up, "I don't think I will ever forget that sound."

"Hey, I was thinking at the ceremony on Thursday," Wils moves the conversation away, "What did you think about her telling everyone she was pregnant? I mean, if that was me I would not say anything until I was back home."

"Yeah, it was like she wanted somebody there to know," Ferriss added.

They saw it as well. However, they would just dismiss it, as she needed someone to blame so she blamed Herndez. Then just like that, I remembered that night at Oskar-Helene Heim while Vela was on Guard Duty at Doughboy City.

WEST BERLIN, GERMANY • US SECTOR • OSKAR-HELENE HEIM BAHNHOF • IMBISS STAND • SEPTEMBER 11, 1989 • MONDAY • 2130HRS

I had just left Ann's house in the American Housing Area. She had a test to study for so I was not going to be staying any later. Besides, we have the weekend. I made my way down to the bus stop that I needed to be at to take the right bus back to McNair. While I waited for the bus to arrive, it was time for a little late night snack.

"Ein bratwurst mit pommes bitte" I told the Imbiss attendant. The late night snack of German sausage that usually comes with a small roll and French fries with mayonnaise. While waiting for my food, which is just a couple of minutes at most, I start watching the late evening activity at the corner of Clayallee and Argentinische Allee.

The intersection of Clayallee and Argentinische Allee is at the heart of the American community in West Berlin. At the intersection was the US Berlin Command Headquarters, US Shopping Center, Family Housing Area, Berlin American Community schools, a Tank Company, bowling alley and the Commissioned Officer and Non-Commissioned Officer Clubs.

After receiving my food order, I moved over to a bench in front of the Imbiss (snack) stand, which gave me a better view on life in this corner of Berlin. As it was just minutes after 9:30 in the evening the vehicle and pedestrian traffic was rather light. As I ate my meal, I noticed a familiar face go walking by at a fast pace. I also saw that there is something not familiar on that face, the face is that of a female who was crying. The crying face belonged Vela's wife. The same Private Vela that is on Guard Duty at this very moment back in Doughboy City.

Asking myself, "Now, why would she be out and why would she be crying?"

No sooner than I asked myself that question, I see someone else even more familiar come out of the train station. It was Staff Sergeant Herndez. Not wanting to be seen, I quickly ducked back into the shadow while Herndez scanned the area obviously looking for someone. He gave up looking and started to walk towards the Imbiss just as the Berlin BVG #10 bus came through the intersection of Clayallee and Argentinische Allee. Herndez turned and walked to the bus stop just outside the U-Bahnhof in time to hop on board and make the trip back to the barracks. I was saved by the very much on-time schedule of the BVG, had the bus been held up by one light or a slow driver and I might have been discovered. However, my celebration may have been a bit premature, as he was making his way to the back of the bus Herndez looked out the back window. He did a quick double take and for one very long second we made eye contact. Well, it felt like eye contact. Sometimes you can see out the back of the buses but when it first gets moving, you just want to make sure you do not fall flat on your face.

The number 10 bus route took passengers from Oskar-Helene-Heim Bahnhof down Clayallee into the heart of the Zehlendorf district of Berlin. The heart of the district located at the intersection of Clayallee, Berliner Strasse, Potsdamer Strasse, and Teltowerdamm otherwise known as "girl-watcher's corner." The Bus continued on Teltowerdamm until it made left on Goerzallee and straight on to the main gate at McNair Barracks and all points east of the Four Ring or Platz des 4.Juli. This was one of the most popular bus routes in the American Sector of Berlin. It connected the GIs based at McNair to the main Headquarters for the US Occupation Forces of Berlin and the Oskar-Helene Heim train station. The train station was a straight shot to downtown West Berlin. The 1989 BVG U2 line took its passengers from the outer fringes of the southwestern part of the city right to the heart of the shopping and tourist center of West Berlin, the Kurfürstendamm otherwise known by its nickname the Ku'damm by the locals.

I took the last bite of the bratwurst, threw away the paper plate, then walked back to the corner and looked down Argentinische Allee to where Vela's wife was walking. I saw her cross the road and walk down the street into the military housing area. I turned back to walk to the bus stop to wait for the next number 10 bus.

"Guerra…Specialist Guerra…Guerra!"

"Huh?" snapping back from the memory of that night.

"When do you want to go to the East? It will be October and they are playing those commercials, on AFN, about sending Christmas packages back soon so they get there on time. I want to get my mother some stuff from the East," Wils, as always, thinking ahead, made a good point another reason to be away from the unit for the day.

"Yeah, our supply of Stolichnaya is running low," from the table next to them Sergeant Randall Summit chimed in.

"Sergeant Summit, if you drive us over, I'll buy you that case of Stoli" I was eager to seize the opportunity to ride over to East Berlin. It sure beats walking.

"You mean that?"

"Of course, at a $1.50 a bottle it is the best investment ever, especially since none of us will have to carry it along with the stuff we buy. Not like the last time we went, between the four of us there were three cases."

"Alright, let me talk to Barbie, she'll say yes"

"Whipped! You mean like ask for permission, Sgt. Summit?"

"Settle down, Specialist"

"Hey, I call them like I see them Sergeant"

By the end of the day, Sgt. Randall Summit got his wife's permission then the five of us settled on the day after tomorrow. We got the platoon sergeant's verbal approval and began filling out the "East Pass". The "East Pass" short for 'Request for Travel to East Berlin' form, a one-page form, used to track who is going to be in the Soviet Sector of Berlin, vehicle type, and approving authority signature. The form was left with the Military Police at Checkpoint Charlie, where they would stamp the form with the time the travelers went across and keep the form until they returned. This was to ensure that any member of the US Army that was in East Berlin was accounted for should there a need or special circumstance arise.

CHAPTER NINE

WEST BERLIN, GERMANY • US SECTOR • PARKS RANGE • INCIDENT LOCATION 89-067A • OCTOBER 2, 1989 • MONDAY • 1330HRS

The members of 2nd Platoon and 3rd Platoon made our way off the bus and took the long walk through Doughboy City. The CID Investigators wanted to do another walkthrough concerning where we were during the accident. It was obvious that none of us really wanted to be there but we were glad we did not have to road-march through the cobblestone back streets of Berlin to get to Doughboy City.

The purpose was to put all of us in our places and to determine if all of the human remains that could be collected were and to see if anyone's memory gets jogged enough to provide a new insight into the situation. Ultimately, the lead investigator, CID Special Agent M. Emmett knew this was just a simple open and close case. As it happened in West Berlin, so close to the border, in a training area, OCONUS (Outside the Continental United States), the report had to be cleared by the French, Brits, and even the Soviets before it could be released. All the T's and I's had better be dotted and crossed, though not necessarily in that order but it had to be done.

Once my group reached the site, the investigators gave everyone instructions to go to the positions we were at that foggy morning last week. Once we were in position, the interviews began from left to right with 2nd Platoon going first, then down the line to 3rd Platoon. During the conversations with the CID investigators nothing new was revealed, everyone was either filling a sandbag or standing watch with their weapon. The watching and waiting was for something to happen in front of their fighting positions.

When Special Agent Emmett arrived at our position he asked, "OK, now you understand this is just a follow-up interview to hopefully discover something all of us may have overlooked. Sometimes, the most mundane can be what breaks a case wide open. So let's begin, where were the two of you at the time of the explosion?"

I started, "Back there," pointing to the tree line, "filling sandbags. I was bringing one of the last ones and setting it in place when…that was it. When it went off. And like I said, it knocked me down, it knocked down the sandbags. I thought that Ferriss, I thought that some of the sandbags fell on top of him and I saw a shoulder so I tried to wake him up but it wasn't him."

"Yeah, that's what I saw too." Ferriss adds, "Just a lot of fog and sandbags and something there. I was wondering who he was talking to because it wasn't me. I wasn't there, the blast wave blew me over a couple of feet."

"It was really hazy in the fog, but we got up and then we saw the arm and not body and that was when we called for a medic. It was like all hell broke loose then. Everyone started calling for a medic," I said.

"So, you were the one filling the sandbags?" the CID Investigator asked.

"Yes, sir, I was."

"Tell me, while you were filling sandbags, where were you digging?"

I walked over to where I was filling the sand bags and where I was digging the hole for the dirt to fill the sandbags. It is easier to take dirt out from a hole than to dig fresh from the top each time the shovel is put to the ground.

The Investigator looks around and says, "Now this was further back than from where Private Vela was digging."

"Yes, yes normally we are a little further back from the position, that way if someone is looking with binos they would not see us digging, filling sandbags, and then moving them only to give away the location of our position."

"OK, so it's quite a way to haul sandbags?"

"Yes it is, but we are training and if we don't do it now and when the time comes to really do it, it may mean our lives."

"So it was just you back here?"

"Yes, I could not see anyone around me but I could hear people talking, shovels digging in the dirt and I could hear people cursing."

"What did you hear?"

"Well, when we first started filling sandbags, everybody was complaining about the roots, everybody was complaining about why here in the tree line? But it all calmed down when they finally broke through the roots and got into the dirt, that's nice dirt."

"Then as the morning progressed?"

"Well, the fog got thicker, but we kept working. I got off track one time but I finally figured that if I stay close to the trees I would get back to our position with no problem."

"Where did you go?"

"I just ended up in front of everybody and I realized that I walked too far down."

"And then?"

"Nothing I just came back up found my spot and got back to work."

"OK, did you hear anybody else get lost or anything?"

"No, I really didn't hear much. Just people talking as the morning went on, we were getting bored waiting for the assault to begin."

The investigator asked, "What do you mean by bored, were they getting antsy, were just goofing around?"

"No, no, no, it wasn't like that. It was just we had already completed our positions and were just sitting there waiting for the fog to lift. Word came down that we were ready to go but were going to wait for the fog to start to lift because it was just too thick. I do not blame them, I mean, I would not want to run smack into a building. You know go full speed down this hill and run into a wall or one of the burned out vehicles, or worse still a triple strand of concertina wire, someone is not going to sleep too good. At night, you can tell where the fire barrels are but once daylight hits it's all good. However, when it is foggy you cannot tell exactly where you are especially when the sun lights it all up. So I don't blame them for wanting to wait but the waiting is the hardest part."

"Tom Petty...nice." Agent Emmett recognizing the song reference, "OK, then what happened?"

"Well, then we got the word to reinforce our fronts. I was like more of this sandbag bullshit! I mean come on, what more did they want us to do? It was supposed to be a hasty position, just enough to slow down the bullets, and that is all. Yet, they wanted us to reinforce the front. It made sense, they wanted us to stay busy, awake, and not fall asleep and not do anything. Trust me, I was ready to go to sleep. I know Ferriss, well, let's say that I heard some sawing logs coming from his AO (area of operations)."

"OK then, was this right before?"

"Yes, yes I was starting to fill the sandbags. I was looking at putting another row, another wall of about 24 sandbags and I got about through the eighth one when that was it. When it went off. "

"Twenty-four isn't that a lot?"

"Well, it is eight on the base and two more rows on top of that for a total of three rows of eight or twenty four altogether. That was all we needed."

"Oh, OK then what happened?"

"That was it. There was nothing out of the ordinary. I heard Staff

Sergeant Herndez tell Vela to move down. Vela did not want to move because he already had his hole dug. All I was thinking was shit here comes Laffington to move me up and start a new hole."

"What do you mean Staff Sergeant Herndez told him to move up?"

"Yeah, he just told him to move closer to the position, to right where the tree line begins."

"And you could hear him clearly?"

"Yes, I never thought about it but yeah I'm surprised the people down in Doughboy didn't hear Herndez, I mean Staff Sergeant Herndez. I guess he just wanted everybody closer. I do not know. He just told Vela to move up and told him to go over there. I could not see him point where or anything like that. You could hear the voices, he said, 'I need you to move up here a little closer' and Vela was kind of like 'Sergeant I've already started digging here and I am already filling these bags' and that's when Staff Sergeant Herndez said, 'Vela that's a direct order.' So that was pretty much it. I got back to digging and filling the bags. I guess he conformed and went to where Herndez wanted him to go because I didn't hear any more complaining or bitching or moaning. I know he walked to where Herndez wanted him because I didn't hear any digging coming from where he was."

"So that was pretty much it, you filled your sandbags, the mortars went off and that was it?"

"That's all I remember Agent Emmett. I don't remember much of anything else. Just a boom, a terrible moan mixed in with the explosion and that was it. Then people yelling for Medic! That was it. It was crazy."

"OK, listen, if you remember anything else or think you saw something and I know that the fog was thick I was here that morning. I was driving in and yes, I know. So don't sweat that. Again, if something just pops up, you remember hearing something, something different or someone saying something else just let me or any of the other Agents know."

"Yes sir, if I remember something but like I said that was it. The only thing out of the ordinary was Laffington not showing up to tell me to move up. And I was not ready to start digging a new hole."

"OK, alright Specialist Thank you. That will be all."

"Can I go over there and just take a look?" I was referring to the blast site.

"I know that the crime tape is down but try not to disturb anything, especially, the hole just in case we need to refer to it during the rest of the interviews," with that Agent Emmett walked over to the next position.

As I approached the blast site, I was still in disbelief of what happened, how it all went down and how quickly our friend's life ended. In my mind, I was recapping the events of that day from the banging on the doors when the CQ activated the Alert notification to the Ambulance taking the pieces of PFC David Vela away forever from Doughboy City and from Berlin. I could not remember anything different, anything out of the ordinary, I could not find anything different, my memory keeps playing it out just the way I heard it through the fog.

I stopped in front of the blast crater trying to imagine where Vela was standing and shoveling at the time of the blast. I started looking around. To the north, northeast and just down the hill is Doughboy City. The mock town that the US Army in Berlin used to create and write the book on modern urban warfare, combat in the cities, military operation in urbanized terrain (MOUT). Things that happened and were taught in Doughboy would be the basis for any urban action the US Armed Forces would undertake in any future conflict. However, today it was just a sad, cold, and lonely place.

I looked to the North and saw the 3rd Platoon line and saw the other investigators talking to the others in the platoon. I see Ferriss talking to Special Agent Emmett. Down below, at the base of the hill I see the bus, ready to go. I scan again towards Doughboy City. I was thinking about the concrete city that is heaven and hell to some people, actually it is heaven and hell to everybody. It is a nice place when you are not doing anything, hunkered down for the evening and a fire barrel is going, it is so nice. When you are trying to fill sandbags and build a fighting position in 32 degree Fahrenheit wet and windy weather it is pure hell.

However, when the evening comes to Doughboy City, quickly, fire barrels are lit. The fire barrels are actually 55-gallon drums with the top removed and a fire on the inside. The heat that barrel gives off is fantastic and when your fellow soldiers gather around it, well, those are some of the best times. Many years from now, I will remember and know that nothing would compare to those simple times. When all the action for the day has ceased and it was just soldiers and no outside influence, just Infantrymen. They could be themselves, they could let their guard down, just shoot "the shit" or vent about the bad and celebrate the good as we gathered around a single 55-gallon drum with a roaring fire on the inside. There would never be another time like that. For now, I was dealing with the passing of a friend and I was starting to think it was not an accident. Where was a fire barrel when you needed one?

I continued looking around, to the south where 1st Platoon's positions were and where the ground assault forces were going to be launching the attack on the mock city. I turned and looking to the south beyond the positions and saw the wooded area. A little to the south and to west I see the tree line. Continuing to scan from south to southwest, I can see beyond the trees to the West Berlin – East German frontier fence. I see the agriculture fields that are neatly tilled but never seem to grow anything.

I continued scanning the area but not really looking for anything in particular, I thought about Vela and know that he didn't see much either. The last thing he saw was heat, that white engulfing heat and the fog. I was looking towards the southwest corner of the Parks Range complex and saw the East German Guard Tower with a clear unobstructed view. I had been out there numerous times since arriving in Berlin and I have never noticed that the view from the guard tower had a straight shot to the blast spot and beyond that to the "warehouse" where some "items" were stored and some "events" took place. I wonder if they knew about it. Yeah, I almost forgot where I was. I was in Berlin and in Berlin everyone makes it a point to know where you go, when you go, and just how much you gave when you went. Surely, they knew. They had to know.

As I continued looking across to the west, I saw a US Army issue GP Medium Olive Drab (Army Green) tent that was erected after the explosion. The tent was set up by the US Army EOD personnel to be used as a staging area for when they came to sweep the area to look for any stray rounds that were still laying around.

The last report from the Explosive Ordinance Disposal staff was an "all clear" but how far do the detectors search down? The CID investigators also set up their shop for any fieldwork they needed to do. There were people on the site 24 hours a day since that morning, keeping it secure especially from visitors that may come from across the fence. They sometimes come across to get a closer look or for some other reason. I continues scanning towards the west when I stop.

I looked back at the East German Guard Tower and said aloud, "it's a clear view."

At this point, I was just staring at the tower. Obviously, they were looking back. They always look back. They were looking through binoculars and no doubt, a photograph or two was taken by now. Those East Germans never missed a beat and were quick to photograph anyone they caught looking at the towers or walking around with or without a camera. After a few seconds of looking at each other, Special Agent Emmett approaches.

"Yeah, we saw that too but the only problem is that they didn't see anything as well."

"Yes, the fog," Guerra asks, "Would they have helped if there was no fog?"

"Hey, anything to make us, the others allies, and in time even the Soviets, they will make everyone look bad. They are more than happy to help. They did it in the past and they will do it again. Anything to further their cause."

"Huh? What do you mean?"

"Well I can't get into it but let's say they have helped us solve some crimes and they have also told us of some things they have done with the aid of some of our own troops."

"Oh, I get it. Anything to make us look bad, I gotcha."

"Yes and they will but not in this case. They have not said anything. We know they heard it and they probably thought all hell was breaking loose and we were cutting through the fence. Whoever was on duty that morning probably, also thought that they were caught in the middle of something they did not want to be caught in the middle of whatever was happening."

"Yeah, I understand I don't want to be in the middle of this either."

"Well, whether we like it or not, we are all deep up to our necks in the middle of this one. All right, we are all just about done. Come on, let's get everyone formed up and on the bus so you can get your early weekend started especially after this past week."

"Yeah, I could use a Guinness down at the Irish Pub." I said.

As I gave the area one last look around, my eyes scanned past the Guard Tower, and something in one of the windows catches my attention. However, when I looked back the window was open but there was nothing or no one in it. I was not too sure of what I saw. It was like a flash of light or a reflection of the sun off a mirror or something shiny. Then again, it might just be stress of these past several days. As I started walking down the hill, I turned one last time. There it was, there they were, one of the guards was crowding the window and holding something shiny in front of him. It may have been a watch or a pocket watch. It was as if he really wanted me to see it but just as quickly as he filled up the guard tower's window, he and whatever he was holding were gone from view.

I really did not think much about it. Sometimes, they want to trade and sometimes they want to get you in trouble. I heard that one time, they recorded the entire conversation of a jogger, who happened to be a clerk in one of the support units from Andrews Barracks. They wanted American Coca-Cola in trade for belt buckles and other uniform items. Well, the clerk had the soda pop and they gave him a box containing nothing but stacks of counterfeit British Pound notes. The film was edited to show the soldier handing over tubes containing film canisters with "classified" microfilm and being paid off. Then the unit clerk was declared *persona non grata*, busted down to E-1, charged with conspiracy with an enemy agent, a court martial, and the last anyone heard about him was that he was in Kansas making small rocks out of big rocks. Whether it is true or not, one thing is certain all rumors have some truth in them.

I got on the bus. After a while, everyone made their way onto the bus and we were on our way back to McNair. Still in a state of mourning and under the threat of Congressional investigation we were given the rest of the week off to be on standby should the CID need anything further to close out their investigation. On the way back, Special Agent Emmett told those of us that were going to East Berlin to be careful. It was a little weird what these guys knew. I guess Command had to clear it with CID before we could go over.

CHAPTER TEN

EAST BERLIN, GERMANY • USSR SECTOR • ALEXANDERPLATZ • OCTOBER 4, 1989 • WEDNESDAY • 1000HRS

"Alright, where are we going first?" Sgt. Randall Summit asked Ferriss, Wils and myself as we made our way to the shopping center of East Berlin which also happens to be the de facto center of East Berlin, Alexanderplatz. The Alex, as the locals call it, is not only home to one of Europe's most famous train stations but also the home of the pride and joy of the East German hierarchy: Der Fernsehturm.

The Fernsehturm is an East German television tower that was completed in 1969 and at 368 meters tall, it is the tallest structure in both German nations combined and at the time is the fourth tallest structure in all of Europe. This needle with a ball on top can be seen from the Grunewald in the far western side of West Berlin and just about from any other point in the city. It stands shooting up into the East Berlin sky as a symbol of what? No one is sure, the East Germans say one thing and on a sunny day, those in the west say something else. The thing is that when the sun shines on the spire the design of the ball shaped design creates the effect of a crucifix on the ball. Those in the West call it the "Rache des Papstes" or "Pope's Revenge."

Mixed among the history, pageantry, and propaganda is technology. The technology at Alexanderplatz comes in the form of several hundred live closed circuit cameras, motion detection cameras, and time delay still cameras. All scattered throughout the Alex mounted on sides of buildings, behind billboards, in parked cars, inside buildings, behind glass, and even on people of which some are Stasi or Stasi informants. On any given day, there is a very good chance that the majority of the people you see walking around are a spy, a plant, a mole, an informant, a potential spy and in the case of the children, future spies.

Every member of the US Army in Berlin, while having free access to the city of East Berlin or the Soviet Sector of Berlin, receives a briefing before entering that sector on what to do, what not to do, how to behave, and whom to call for when trouble arises. Above all, everyone is reminded not to recognize the authority of the East German military force as they are not recognized as a valid entity in East Berlin by the US, French, and British Armies of Occupation. If there is any trouble, a Soviet Officer or Liaison must be present and we are to only speak to the Soviet Liaison requesting they make contact with the members of the US Military at Checkpoint Charlie.

This practice is to ensure that only members of the Army of Occupation of Berlin can address any issue with any member of the Army of Occupation, no matter the Allied country of origin. Of course, things happen in East Berlin just as they happen in any other city in the world. Things such as traffic accidents and sudden illness causing soldiers or their family members to panic and turn what would a simple situation into an international incident that quickly gets the East German military and government involved. It has happened and it will happen again. Once a situation occurs and the East Germans get involved words like "spies" and "saboteurs" are quickly thrown around and soon family members are sent packing back to the United States. This of course, takes place after long drawn out explanations and diplomatic assurances that the individuals involved were not there to commit any act other than trying to buy some souvenirs at the Kaufhof or enjoy a fine meal at the Moskau Restaurant.

Once the four of us stepped onto the grounds of Alexanderplatz proper, in the shadow of the Alexanderplatz Bahnhof, we could almost instantly feel that all eyes were on us, the Americans. Of course, it is common for US, British, or French troops to be in East Berlin, and yet we are still viewed as a novelty. We are also viewed as a symbol of something those from the East cannot have and that is Freedom. Then again, others eye the Americans and the rest of the Westerners, as something that is wrong in the world. No matter what the reason, people are always watching.

As we walked across the concrete yard, we made our way to the Kaufhof department store. This is one of the few stores in East Berlin that was always kept well stocked and excellent service is always provided, thus the infamous "long lines" are kept to a minimum. Well-stocked and small lines are something that the rest of East Berlin, East Germany or any member nation of the Warsaw Pact cannot boast. Aside from those specialty shops scattered throughout the "Alex" the Kaufhof was designed to be the shopping focal point of East Berlin. They had just about anything the "big spender" from the West could ever want from the East. If they did not have it then it was not available anywhere among the Warsaw Pact nations. They were that good and they were that popular, not just with the Military Forces based in West Berlin but also with the diplomatic and press corps that inhabited the capital of East Germany and those assigned to West Berlin.

Once inside the department store, we agreed to split up but meet in the men's department on the third floor in an hour. This would allow all of us time to fill our Christmas shopping lists and have a little time to fill our personal shopping lists, as well. Which for me was wool socks. For some odd reason, I really like the East German wool socks, as they seem to work better at keeping my feet warm on those cold days and nights in the Grunewald and Doughboy City, after road marching, of course. I made that mistake once and my feet have never forgiven me for that.

My list was relatively short, so I finished before everyone else. I had a few minutes to kill and wanted to check out the sports department when the camping gear caught my eye. I stopped and scanned the unique offerings from the DDR, Poland, Czechoslovakia, Yugoslavia, USSR, and even China. I found a few Romanian walking sticks and thought they would do well at keeping the werewolves at bay. Maybe even, help to do that "Transylvania Twist." Whether they really work at keeping the wolves at bay or just helping me get up a hill, they are very nice to look at, nonetheless.

While looking at the walking sticks, someone approaches and asks in a heavy German accent, "Ich helfen sie kann?"

"Oh no, I am just looking." I respond in English without thinking to answer in German.

"Please excuse me, I did not know you only spoke English," said the German attendant, whose nametag read UWE. Interesting name.

"That's OK."

"Are you British or American?"

"I am American"

"Yes, yes American, I forget your uniform color, entschuldigen Sie bitte"

"machts nichts"

"Ah, Sprechen sie Duetsche?" His eyes lit up, it seems that all Germans like it when visitors to their countries speak German. They get more personable, a little more open, friendlier, and that is a good thing especially when trying to establish a common bond with the people that are in a nation your country has sent you to occupy.

"Ein bisschen. A little bit, I am still learning. Ich lerne Deutsch."

"Well it is very gute"

"And so is your English. Did you learn it in school?"

"Yes, they teach us English and Russian. Because I nichts vergessen I mean I do not forget English I can work here helping."

"Sehr gute!"

"How can I help you?"

"How much for this Spazierstock?"

"Yes, that is a fine Romanian Walking stick and that is 27 East Marks."

"I will take it."

As we make our way towards the cashier station, I saw someone off to the side near the portable field stoves standing there and looking at me and the clerk, while looking at what appears to be a notebook. I quickly dismissed it as a Stasi, CIA, or some other intelligence spook keeping tabs on the East German and me. Then again, it could just be the Floor Concierge making certain that a good presentation is made for the American.

"That will be 27 East Marks."

As I start for my right front pocket, I look down and right in front of me I saw a hand, a wrist, and a silver metallic watch. Then a voice caught me off guard, "Herr Guerra."

"Yes?" I took one-step back and get into a defensive stance. Uncertain of what is going on and why this man has called me by my last name. I was not wearing my nametag on my Class A Coat, as it is not part of the uniform when travelling in the Soviet Sector of Berlin. My dog tags were under my shirt as they are part of the uniform, all the time.

"Do not be alarmed…there is nothing wrong," the man with a definitive German accent in his English says in a low tone so as not to attract attention.

That however, is too late, as the cashier has already started walking away from the cashier station. This may be his way of distancing himself from any impending trouble that usually accompanies individuals that all of a sudden have their name called. I guess working in East Berlin, the clerk has plenty of experience in knowing when to walk away.

"How do you know my name?" I asked.

"You are American Army Specialist Guerra?"

"I don't know who you are, I need to go" and with that I leave my unfinished purchase behind and make a beeline straight for the escalator up to the third floor. Remembering we were to meet in the Men's Department.

As I was leaving the area, I kept looking back to the individual at the counter. He was still looking at me. I kept an eye on him until I was a few feet from the top of the escalator on the third floor. Once there I make a quick scan and see what appears to be the men's clothing department a sign in German "Herren-Abteilung" confirms that I am in the right area. Making my way towards that part of the store, I stop dead in my tracks by someone calling my name again.

Sgt. Randall Summit says, "Guerra, I thought you'd still be shopping."

"Holy Crap, Sgt. Summit you're not going to believe what just happened?"

"What happened?"

"I was downstairs where the camping gear is and just as I was about to pay this guy came up to me and called me by my name."

"And?"

"And nothing I got the fuck outta there and here I am."

"Did you talk to anyone?"

"Just the clerk who was ringing me up for the walking stick. Once that guy showed up the clerk got out of the AO in a hurry."

"Alright, let's wait here for everyone and we'll get out of this store."

"Has that ever happened to you, Sgt. Summit?"

"Never and this is not good that it happened to you."

"What do you mean?"

"They know your name," Summit said without any emotion. Summit and I both knew that once they know your name either they had something on you or they were going to get something from you. It was just that simple, either way it meant something very bad was going to happen. Later, Sgt. Summit would tell me that the only thing he found odd was that they did not attempt to have a longer conversation with me or set up a future meeting. Of course, as all this was going down all I could think was we are going to have to report this to the MPs at Checkpoint Charlie.

A few minutes later, Wils and Ferriss met up with us. Each lugging quite a few boxes and bags thus they were more than ready to leave Kaufhof and drop off the packages in Summit's family station wagon. Then off to lunch and the last stop of the day, the state run duty free and liquor store for the ever-abundant Stolichnaya Vodka straight from Mother Russia. At what comes out to be $1.50 a bottle the Westerners tended to be spoiled when it came to exploiting that which the Communist system had worked so hard to make.

After a fine lunch at the Restaurant "Moskau" on one of East Berlin's most famous streets, Karl-Marx-Allee, it was a short walk down a few blocks and crossing the street, we turn onto a side street, Otto-Braun Strasse, and there it was. Set among the Soviet style buildings, a simple entrance with a glass showcase next to it. This shop was obviously one that was frequented by the Westerners as it had plenty of merchandise and very few East German shoppers.

When we made our purchases, we started walking back to where Summit had parked his vehicle. It was not that far but before crossing Karl-Marx-Allee again. Out of a dark corner of a gray building, they were all gray, someone approached us and spoke in broken English, "You want, buy Russian watch. Is military watch." He holds it up in from of him as is he is trying to block others from seeing what he is doing.

Sgt. Summit quickly responds, "Nein, raus!"

The German then stepped in front of me and asked, "You buy, bitte?"

"Nein"

"Herr Guerra, please buy this"

I was taken back, again, when I was called by my name. This time, everyone heard him call my name.

"Hey, how do you know his name?" asks Wils.

"Uh, I am sorry I must go, entschuldigen Sie, bitte" and with that the East German flashes Guerra the watch one more time and leaves.

The others start to go after him but Summit tells them stop and leave him alone. It definitely will be more trouble than what it worth is. "Hell, they probably already know all our names." Summit added, "Come on let's get back across."

As we start to finally make our way towards the Summit's family station wagon, I begin to replay what just happened and wonder why two East Germans were calling me by my last name. Then as I was remembering, just how adamant the East German was about showing me the watch. It looked familiar, almost like the watch that the other German was wearing in the Sporting Goods department at the Kaufhof. At that same moment I remembered that afternoon, at Doughboy City, when I thought I saw someone that was going out of his way to show me a watch, as if to trade.

I continue to replay the events of today and those at Doughboy City, I was starting to put two and two together. Could these two East Germans be the same two soldiers that were in the guard tower? The watch and the stance that the last German took reminds me of how the Border Guard stood in that window as if to block what he was showing when he was flashing that watch. Could it be merely a coincidence? I do not think so. After being in Berlin for these many months, I have concluded that in the Walled City there is no such thing as a coincidence. Let me clarify, there is no such thing as random coincidence only intentional coincidence.

WEST BERLIN, GERMANY • US SECTOR • CHECKPOINT CHARLIE • MP HUT • OCTOBER 4, 1989 • WEDNESDAY • 1502HRS

"Let me get this straight. You were at the Kaufhof when someone approached you and called you by your name, and you never said your name to anyone?" The senior MP on duty is filling out an Incident Report based on the information that I was providing.

Already frustrated for repeating the entire story for the third time, at Checkpoint Charlie alone, I replied, "Yes, sir."

"And a different individual outside the liquor store?"

"Yes, sir."

"OK, you do understand that if you get approached again you are to notify your chain of command? Also you should be hearing from someone at MI or CID by close of business tomorrow about this."

"Yes, sir!" I think to myself that I am going to have to repeat the entire incident numerous times before this is all said and done.

"OK, you are good to go, remember report anything strange immediately."

"Thank you, sir" as I come to the position of attention, salute, and exit the hut that serves as Checkpoint Charlie.

"All clear?" Specialist Wils asked as we start to get into Sgt. Summit's station wagon.

"Yep, he said that CID or MI would be talking to me tomorrow."

"What about? Are you confined to the barracks?"

"Not that I know of...I mean I plan on meeting Ann tonight at the Ku'dorf"

"Alright everyone buckle up!" Sgt. Summit called out just before pulling onto Friedrichstrasse and hitting the Berlin streets that will eventually take us through the American sector all the way back to McNair Barracks.

CHAPTER ELEVEN

WEST BERLIN, GERMANY • US SECTOR • McNAIR BARRACKS • 6th BATTALION 502nd INFANTRY • HEADQUARTERS • STAFF DUTY OFFICER • OCTOBER 4, 1989 • WEDNESDAY • 1735HRS

"Specialist Guerra, what is going on?" asked Lt. Daniel Barony, the evening's Staff Duty Officer, the Battalion's Officer in Charge for the evening until he is relieved in the morning. He is the Battalion Commander's on site representative until the proper chain of command arrives, which is typically the start of the next business day.

I proceeded to explain the day's events for the fourth and most definitely not the last time. I tried not to embellish too much. Then again, there really is not anything I could exaggerate about other than the fact the entire day was surreal. It got to the point that I was starting to wonder if it was not someone on this side of the wall that was trying to test anyone or me that was travelling in East Berlin today. I made certain to include the debriefing at Checkpoint Charlie with the Military Police Officers.

"Well sounds like you had an interesting day. CID called before you arrived to stress that you are not confined to quarters but they would like for you to check in every hour or so if you decide to go outside the gate [of McNair Barracks]. The Battalion Commander did not say you were confined to the barracks but I would recommend you stay close. Either at Andrews, BB Compound, or Truman Plaza or here and not go downtown."

"I can deal with that. I thought for sure it was going to be bad, Sir." I said.

I am starting to feel that something bigger than me was going on all around but I just could not put my finger on it.

"Well Specialist Guerra, it could be worse. We could be packing your gear for you and you would be at the RTO (Rail Transportation Office) waiting for the Duty Train to pull out of here tonight. So if I were you I would consider myself lucky."

"Yes, most definitely, sir."

"OK, you can return to your unit and don't forget to check in with Staff Sergeant Williams, he's got the duty with me tonight."

"Yes, sir."

"That is all, dismissed."

"I will check in, thank you sir." I come to attention, salute the Infantry Officer, do an about face, and walk out of the Staff Duty Office.

I started questioning everything, 'Holy crap what the hell is going on? How did they know my name? What's the deal?' I continued to ask myself those questions all the way back to the first floor, where the Alpha Company area is located.

As I passed the Charge of Quarters (CQ) desk, I see SSG Herndez is the CQ for the night. Great. Just as Herndez sees me, he starts to put one of his big shit eating grins on his face, stands up, and opens his mouth, "Well, well, well Specialist Guerra, I take it you saw the SD NCO?"

I stop and comes to attention, knowing that anything less with SSG Herndez would be asking for more hell from this individual, I reply, "Yes, SSG Herndez and also with the Staff Duty Officer, Sergeant."

"So what did they want Specialist?"

"I had an incident in the East and they wanted me to debrief them?"

"Well, don't stand there like an asshole, tell me what happened?" Herndez got even closer and tried to exert the power of his rank on me. I was not budging.

"Staff Sergeant Herndez, I have been told not to talk about this with anyone until the investigation is over."

"Now who told you this Specialist?"

"The Officer at Checkpoint Charlie, the Staff Duty Officer, and the CID investigator, Sergeant"

Knowing fully well that I would most definitely tell the CID investigator who I have spoken to about the situation, it was wise for Herndez to decide to change the subject, "OK Specialist, you still seeing that hot blonde that I always see you with?"

"Yes, Staff Sergeant." I was quick to reply at the same time I started looking around for a way to get past Herndez.

Herndez leans in and talks in a lower tone so that only I can hear, "Well you let me know when she is ready for a real man, because you know what they say, rank has its privileges."

I looked him right in the eye, knowing fully well what Herndez is talking about and I was ready to rock and roll. Then again, the nonchalant way he said what he said made me believe that he has said this before, to others, and more than likely has acted on it. Herndez stares back at me and then puts a smirk on his face.

While maintaining eye contact I say, "Well to tell you the truth Sergeant, she didn't have to look very far to find a real man because she found me," while returning the smirk.

"We'll see Specialist Guerra, the week is still young."

Now what did he mean by that? I thought to myself. Just as I was about to fire back, the phone rings and with the CQ Clerk out running an errand, SSG Herndez answered, "Alpha Company, Sixth Battalion, Five Oh Second infantry, this line is not secure, Staff Sergeant Herndez speaking, how may I help you?"

Taking that as my queue to leave, I move out of the CQ area quickly and in few seconds, I am back in my room. That evening, I met Ann at the Burger King over at Truman Plaza, told her what went down over in the East. She just laughed at me because all of a sudden, I am at the center of the Cold War universe and I have done nothing wrong. All eyes are on me because I was buying a pair of gray wool socks. Oh well, maybe there was microfilm sewn into them or they were tagged for the son of a prominent member of the East German Politburo.

CHAPTER TWELVE

WEST BERLIN, GERMANY • US SECTOR • McNAIR BARRACKS • 6th BATTALION 502nd INFANTRY • HEADQUARTERS • BATTALION S-2 OFFICE • OCTOBER 5, 1989 • THURSDAY • 0915HRS

The meeting with the Military Intelligence Officer, CID investigator, and the Battalion Intelligence Officer (S-2) was over before it even began. They just needed to hear my side of what happened, again, as well as from the others that were there. Of all the people in the S-2's office, I recognized only the S-2, Captain Daniel Thomas and CID Special Agent Emmett. I thought that as Emmett was already familiar with me and all the men of 2nd and 3rd Platoon of Alpha Company it would be easy to process the debrief in that Emmett had experience questioning us after Vela' death.

The interview had taken no more than 10 minutes and it was straight forward questioning as at this time there was no reason to suspect me of any inappropriate conduct. The consensus was that the East Germans randomly picked me either out of a photograph and I was recognized once we crossed Checkpoint Charlie or they think I might know someone who can provide them something they may want. Either way, the officers in my Chain of Command are in agreement that I did the right thing and those that attempted the contact now know that I am not afraid to confront or overtly avoid them and that I will not be worth any further attempts. They let me know that this will be last of the questioning and I can return to my unit with one only condition.

"You will notify the first Officer you see and your chain of command if they ever try to make contact with you again is that understood Specialist?"

"Yes, sir." I asked, "Uh, Sir, do you think they will try?"

"More than likely not, too many people have already seen their face and they do not want to get burned again, besides they know the heat is on and that we are on alert for them to try something," Major Patrick Callahan,

Counter Intelligence Officer for the Military Intelligence unit in Berlin answered.

"Thank you, sir," as I prepared to leave I breathed a small sigh of relief knowing that I was not being sent to the West. Before going in to the meeting I feared this incident would get me a one-way ticket on the duty train to some unit in West Germany like those guys in 1986 I heard about. I really should be more of a glass is half-full kind of person because I am staying in Berlin. I saluted the ranking officer and exited the S-2's office.

Special Agent Emmett made certain that he walked out right behind me. As the door closed behind us, Emmett reached over to stop me. I turned around and looked Special Agent M. Emmett right in the eye, he saw that I had a puzzled look on my face.

"Guerra, you didn't ask me if they would try again."

"I'm sorry Agent Emmett I don't know what you mean?"

"You didn't ask me if the East Germans or Soviets would try again?"

"Oh, I guess you want me to ask you?"

"Yes"

"OK, will they try to make contact again?"

"You better believe they will, for the next month or so you will be followed. Not by the East Germans but by our spooks waiting to see who follows you or tries to make contact and that my young friend is why you are not on the duty train to some unit in the Zone."

"Agent Emmett can I speak to you for a second?"

"Here walk me to my vehicle."

The two of us walked down to the parking lot between 6th Battalion and the McNair Learning Resource Center. Along the way, I explained to him what happened with SSG Herndez at the CQ Desk the night before.

"He was just so matter of fact about what he was saying. It was like he had said it and done it before."

"Specialist, why are you telling me this?"

"Maybe we shouldn't be talking here. Can we meet someplace else?"

"Is there more?"

"I don't know it's just a feeling I have been getting lately and it's getting stronger."

The 2nd Platoon day room overlooked the parking lot that the CID agent and I were walking in. Little did I know that at that exact moment SSG Herndez was looking out the window from the dayroom and was watching us talk.

"Do you want to come down to the office, we can talk there?"

"Can we do it someplace else?"

"Where would you like to meet Specialist?"

"The imbiss at Oskar-Helene Heim at 1400hrs?"

"Very well at 1400hrs"

"Thank you," I said as Special Agent Emmett was getting into his vehicle.

As I turned around to look behind me, paranoid I guess. I did catch a glimpse of a window on the first floor closing. Then what appeared to be the reflection of someone that looked familiar was in the window as it closed. I quickly made my way to the front entrance of Alpha Company and stepped into the orderly room to see if I could see the 2nd Platoon Day room window. To no avail. I made it back to my room.

Just after lunch, I left on the 10 bus that had a couple of people from McNair on it heading back to the bus stop at the Oskar-Helene Heim bahnhof. Once at the imbiss stand, I ordered the usual, a bratwurst and pommes frites and waited for Agent Emmett. A few minutes after 2:00 pm, he showed up with Agent E. Walter in tow. I spent the next hour telling them all about the incidents that have happened so far, including that drunken conversation on the 10 Bus after the Volksfest.

It was just after 4:00pm that we parted ways. That was it for now.

They now knew what I knew.

CHAPTER THIRTEEN

WEST BERLIN, GERMANY • US SECTOR • McNAIR BARRACKS • 6th BATTALION 502nd INFANTRY • COMPANY A • BARRACKS ROOM • OCTOBER 9, 1989 • MONDAY • 2215HRS

"Well, well, well look what the cat dragged in" I said as Wils made his way back to our shared room after spending the weekend at his girlfriend's apartment the entire four day weekend.

"Yeah, if it wasn't for the Alert tomorrow morning I'd still be there."

"I hear that!"

"Where's Ferriss and Brown?"

"Ferriss went to Andrews Barracks with some guys from Mortar Platoon and Brown is upstairs with some of those guys from HHC." Some things never change and that's a good thing or was it?

"And you why aren't you at your in-law's place?" Wils, making a jab at my relationship with Ann.

Ann and I are serious but right now, she has school to worry about and I have my time in the Army to worry about. So for now, we like the level of serious we have. Besides hanging out at her parent's apartment is a welcomed break from barracks life and they seem to like me. Who knows what the future has in store for the two of us?

"Well, everyone knows there will be an alert in the morning so we called it a night. Heck, I was there every day since Friday."

"Yeah, where did you go Thursday afternoon? They were looking for you?"

"They Who?"

"Well, just Laffington, until Williams told him you had a meeting at Andrews."

So, they thought I was at Andrews Barracks. Good no one has any idea I was over at Oskar-Helene Heim talking to the CID Agents. Funny, the Agents did not say what they were going to do with the information I gave them. Probably nothing. It was just my impression of what I thought I saw and heard. They said Thank You and we left. Then again, they were probably just ready to start their three-day weekend and put some of the past week behind them.

"Oh well, they'll find me in the morning." I told Wils.

"Hey Men!" a few minutes later Ferriss walks into the room. He had spent the evening over at the Country Western bar at Andrews Barracks about a mile and half down the road. Andrews Barracks housed the Berlin Brigade's support units. The MPs lived and worked there, as well as the CID agents. A little bit of a history lesson, Andrews Barracks is located on the grounds of former Prussian Main Military academy (Hauptkadettenanstalt).

"Hey!"

"Guerra, where did you go on Thursday afternoon?" asked Ferriss

"Yeah, Wils just told me that Laffington was looking for me."

"Not just him, earlier today SSG Herndez told me was looking for you on Thursday afternoon but couldn't find you."

"Did he say what he wanted?"

"No, just that he was looking for you. Before you ask, I told him I did not know and that you were probably defecting after that BS with the der Ossies."

"Yeah, they were offering not only the watch but a first round draft pick and an option for two Mortar crewmen to be named later," I decided to mess with him back.

It was nice that people were already making fun of my situation. I guess it is just a coping mechanism, we make fun of something and we move on. In this city, you have to cope and move on. There is just way too much serious stuff happening that if you do not make a joke once in a while you will go bonkers or go AWOL.

"I need to remember that one for the next time some Russian wants to trade for something," said Wils.

"Yeah."

"What did the S-2 say?"

I spent the next ten minutes telling them what happened in the S-2's office and what the CID agent told me about being followed by the Military Intelligence guys to see if they try another attempt. Personally, if their own people are not aware of what is going on they really have a problem over at Stasi (East German Ministry for State Security) -land. Those East Germans were so busy spying on each other, it would be safe to say that they botched this one. Then again, I could be wrong and they really want me for some reason. I mean, they did go to all that trouble to learn my name and pronounce it the right way and that has to be worth something. Right?

"So you are Mr. Popular or should I say Specialist Popular," said Wils.

"Yeah, but what a way to become popular."

"True…well time for lights out?"

"Yeah, oh dark thirty comes pretty early around these parts," as I made my way to the latrine down the hall to get ready to hit the rack. No one else was there and that meant I could have a nice long hot shower. There is no way I would attempt a hot shower after PT or after 5:00pm Friday evenings. These times are rare and you take advantage of them when you can. After completing the three S's (scheisse, shower, & shave), I was back in my room.

The overhead lights were off but Wils' TV was on, Ferriss had his headphones on listening to music on his Sony® Walkman©, probably the Stray Cats, and lo and behold, Brown was out to the world in his bunk. A few minutes later, we would hit our respective bunks, get some sleep and maybe a dream.

ALERT!!! ALERT!!! <<BANG>> <<BANG>> and Monday morning came to the men of Alpha Company, 6th Battalion, 502nd Infantry and to the city of West Berlin, again.

CHAPTER FOURTEEN

WEST BERLIN, GERMANY • US SECTOR • LICHTERFELDE DISTRICT • ROUTE CHARLIE (from McNAIR BARRACKS to PARKS RANGE) • OCTOBER 10, 1989 • TUESDAY • 0525HRS

We were road marching out to Doughboy City, again. This time it was a much more leisurely pace however, that did not really help when we got to the last street heading south from Ostpruessendamm, Schwelmer Strasse. The problem with Schwelmer Strasse is that it is a road completely paved with cobblestones. If you are from the new world and have never walked on cobblestone streets well you are in for a treat the first time you do. Think about what it is like to walk on those streets while wearing army combat boots. That's right you feel every single stone.

"Man, these road marches are for the birds," someone in the cold dark morning talked aloud.

"Nah, they're still asleep," someone from the column of Infantrymen across the street called back.

Everyone within earshot started laughing. It was not a particularly funny remark but it certainly was something that no one was expecting to hear in the early hours.

"At ease, back there. Noise discipline people!" SSG Laffington called out to everyone.

We continued our saunter through the residential district between McNair Barracks and Doughboy City. I could only imagine what it was like to wake up early, look out the living room window and see two columns of soldiers, armed to the teeth, marching down the street. It has to be the most surreal thing to see, even for those that have lived in Berlin all their lives. Personally, after all this time it continues to be surreal for me. I know what we are doing in Berlin and why we are here but it still feel like a dream sometimes.

The battalion arrived at Doughboy City at around 0615, quickly moved into the buildings on the north and western side of the Military Operation in Urban Terrain city. Alpha Company moved into the mock warehouse at the northwestern edge of the Doughboy City. In the westernmost room of the warehouse, you could look out the window and see the hill where Vela met his fate. The blast scar was replaced with freshly laid dirt. Of course, in time, the grass and weeds would return but for all of us that were there the scar would never go away.

Sometime around 0815hrs, the deuce and a half trucks rolled into Doughboy and stopped at our respective company areas. The trucks carried our duffel bags along with the remainder of our field gear. Once they left, a second set of trucks arrived with breakfast. Oh yes, fresh scrambled eggs in mermite containers. Every once in a while, the natural chemicals in cooked eggs would react to the aluminum mermite "bullets" (three in every mermite cooler/heater container) and you would get real GREEN EGGS. There was nothing wrong with them, the eggs were completely edible but their color would go from white and yellow to various shades of green. The first time I saw them was in Basic Training, all I could think was that this is where Dr. Seuss got his idea for his book "Green Eggs and Ham." It really tests your courage as a soldier to eat a plate full of green eggs. Once you overcome that you can pretty much handle anything the Mess Hall will throw at you. We were lucky today, no green eggs. Eggs, bacon, oatmeal, and coffee was on the menu. On a cool, crisp early October morning in Berlin, dining al fresco for breakfast could only be done one way and this was it. Sure, we could all be at the Mess Hall having our made to order omelets but as Infantry soldiers we were taught that sometimes we had to make certain sacrifices and being in Berlin we could live with these kind of sacrifices.

While sitting and eating our morning chow the talk going around was about the weekend's past events on the other side of the Berlin Wall. Seems that someone from first platoon got a call from home telling him about what they had read in the L.A. Times newspaper. In East Berlin and other cities throughout the Deutsches Demokratisches Republik there were protest marches all weekend long. However, this past Sunday the 8th things got a little out of hand when East German Security forces violently broke up a candle-lit protest march in East Berlin.

"Yeah, my father said the paper reported that there were peaceful demonstrations against the East German government and they wanted them to launch real political reforms like Gorbachev did in Russia," said Specialist Eric Hartz.

"Well, that explains all the alerts and road marches," declared PFC Tony

Sherman.

"How?" asked Ferriss who was sitting next to Sherman.

"They want to keep us busy and not at the barracks or asking for time off to go to the East to buy booze and then get mixed up with the protests," replied Sherman.

"We were there last week."

"Yes, but now we can only go with an E-6 or higher and in a group of five or more. You guys were lucky because it changed after you came back."

"Hmmm." I said out loud.

"Yeah, don't flatter yourself. These protests have been brewing all summer long and you know that."

"Simmer down dill weed. Don't flatter yourself. You'd have to be dead six months not to know that our friends on the other side of that fence are having a dose of their medicine shoved down their throats," I replied with a "matter-of-fact" tone.

I never really got along with Sherman, it seems that he had two years of college under his belt before signing up with the US Army. He would have been a nice person to have as a friend but this guy never let an opportunity go by to let anyone know what he thought of you because all you had was a high school diploma. He really liked talking down to people. I had known people like him all my life. Being an Army Brat, I traveled with my brothers to numerous military bases and government postings that my father was assigned. I dealt with the children of Ambassadors, Generals, Congressmen, Top Level Government personnel and there was always one or two at every one of my father's assignments. The weird thing was that it was usually the children of mid-level personnel and not of the top tier people. No matter where they came from I was no stranger to nitwits like Sherman. That may be why he did not like me as well, because he knew I was onto him and what he was doing or trying to do.

"Alright listen up!" The First Sergeant saved the day, "Your Platoon Sergeants have their assignments. We are going to be here a while so let us get to filling sand bags. Be careful, I do not want to have to send you home in a hatbox. Platoon Sergeants take charge of your platoons."

"Alright 1st Platoon you have five minutes to finish eating, police your area, and form up in front of the warehouse," yelled the 1st platoon Platoon Sergeant.

"Third Herd, five minutes, eat, police, and formation in front of the warehouse as well!" Laffington said through his daily dip of Copenhagen© chewing tobacco that was placed neatly between his cheek and gum. How he never choked on it I will never know.

All around me, I heard bitching, moaning, and complaining. The typical sounds of happy soldiers.

FIVE MINUTES LATER

"Alright, third platoon. We are going to be on the defense for this one. We have 36 hours to build hasty fighting positions. We will be building them in the buildings immediately to the south of the warehouse," pointing to the buildings behind him, "2nd platoon is immediately next to us in those buildings. Squad leaders take your squads and assign them their positions."

"Alright 2nd Squad let's go, Guerra, Ferriss you are with us," said Sergeant Summit.

We moved out to the building in front of us. Our position was at the far left of the building one window in front that was facing the attacking force, if that is where they were coming from and one door behind us in case we had to do a hasty withdrawal. There was a concrete floor, cinderblock walls on both sides. Inside the room was old furniture, a few pallets, and strands and strands of concertina wire.

Over the next 12 hours, we filled sandbags and began creating a "fortified" hasty fighting position complete with grenade slumps and a covered exit path. When it was time to get some shuteye that covered exit path would come in handy as it helped keep our body heat trapped so long as our ponchos covered both openings and kept the wind out. We might even get away with firing up a heat tab or two to make some hot coffee.

CHAPTER FIFTEEN

WEST BERLIN, GERMANY • US SECTOR • PARKS RANGE • DOUGHBOY CITY • COMPANY A AREA OF OPERATIONS • OCTOBER 11, 1989 • WEDNESDAY • 1508HRS

We were beat, dead tired. All day yesterday filling sandbags and today as well. Up at 0600 and filling sandbags, chow, then walking the perimeter to figure out what is behind the buildings that were likely to be the avenues of approach the attackers will take and then to fill more sandbags. During lunch, the scuttlebutt was that the 4th Battalion was coming out to attack our positions sometime after 1900 hours then again at first light in the morning. Until they attacked, we were going to fill more sandbags. That is until something interesting happened around 1300 hours.

A Military Police sedan drove onto the grounds of Doughboy City. It was an unusual site to have a functional sedan drive onto the training area. There are plenty of vehicles scattered around the city however, these vehicles are salvaged wrecks none of which are functional. Usually, the MPs would drive out in their Humvee when they had business to conduct in a tactical environment. To have an MP sedan appear onsite means that something serious is going down. Usually, that something serious involving a family matter. However, this time it was not the case.

The MPs asked where the Company Command Post (CP) was located. Of course, PFC Sherman stepped up to give the MPs directions in his usual manner. The look on his face was priceless when the MPs looked him over, gave him a smirk, and said, "That is all, Private," emphasizing on the word "Private" and walked away. Guess they were onto him as well.

A minute or two after arriving at the CP, the company commander's Radio Telephone Operator (RTO) comes out of the building and walks over to the 2nd platoon area. A few seconds after that, the Platoon Sergeant calls for SSG Herndez to head over to the Company CP on the double. A minute or so later, everyone in the area stands stunned watching as Herndez steps into the back of the sedan. No hand cuffs though.

At first, everyone thought something bad had happened back home with someone in SSG Herndez's family. Then as the afternoon wore on, word got out that CID wanted to talk to Herndez. That is when the speculation and rumors jumped into overdrive. Someone went as far as saying that he was leading a smuggling operation in the States and that is why he joined the Army. Someone else said that he had information on who was using drugs in the unit. Still others changed things up and said that he was selling information to the Soviets. The problem with that rumor is that any information any of us, in an Infantry line unit, had was usually very old and no longer valid. What we had to offer either they were aware of or it was so old that to extrapolate any current information would not be beneficial to anyone on any side of the wall. I thought to myself, the only option left was what I told them last week and they were working on it, finally.

Things were quiet especially when 1900 hours came and went. We could hear some activity in the wooded area southwest of our location. That could have been the Opposing Forces (OPFOR) moving in to their assembly area or a very large and very loud pack of grune pigs (feral pigs) rooting around for discarded MRE packages. Our suspicion was confirmed when a flashlight was seen shining down in our direction and the loud audible response, "Damnit, Private Forbes! Kill that light!" It was not a pack of grune pigs.

All remained quiet until around 2015 hours when another deuce and a half truck pulled up. It was him, Staff Sergeant Herndez. He was back and this time he sounded very pissed-off. Herndez was cussing and demanding to know the truck driver's name and rank. It seems that the driver stopped in front of the company area and when Herndez jumped off the back of the truck, he landed feet first into a pile of unraveled concertina wire. He was livid as the truck drove off probably back to McNair for the night. Someone called out in the dark.

"Sergeant Herndez, don't move we'll get you out."

"Hurry up! Damn it!"

"At ease, with the noise," Staff Sergeant Laffington said to everyone that was talking.

Might as well had all of us turn on our flashlights. Our positions were slowly starting to be revealed with all the talking that was going on. A few seconds later, the sound of people scuffling out on the wire could be heard. There were at least two others helping Herndez stop his dance with the concertina. You had to be careful getting out of it because that razor wire can easily slice open skin and leave some very nasty cuts. As any

Infantryman that has ever worked with concertina wire will not only tell you but show you, as well.

"Who the fuck is next to us, over there?" asked SSG Herndez as they freed him and were making their way back to the 2nd platoon area.

"That's third platoon sergeant," said someone who sounded a lot like Specialist Tony Garon.

"No shit, Sherlock. I mean who in third platoon is over there? In what order?"

I did not hear the answer as they quieted down. I guess they finally decided to observe light and noise discipline. As 10 o'clock in the evening rolled around that meant "quiet time" was in effect. Quiet time or "Ruhezeit", in German, was that time in the evening until morning when loud noise was not permitted. For us, that meant that no grenade, artillery, tank simulators would go off with their loud report which in essence meant that training came to a halt at 2200 hours. My cohorts and I had no problem with that. Early to bed and even earlier to rise. When any Infantryman can get a night's sleep, even if it is on top of a layer of sandbags life is good. The guard shift had been set, Ferriss and I were on from 0515 to wake up at 0600. Being the last two on guard was always a good thing. It meant you were one of the few that just like the good citizens of Berlin had a good few hours of uninterrupted sleep before all hell broke loose, again.

WEST BERLIN, GERMANY • US SECTOR • PARKS RANGE • DOUGHBOY CITY • ALPHA COMPANY AREA OF OPERATIONS • OCTOBER 11, 1989 • WEDNESDAY • 2241HRS

"Ferriss" a whispering voice breaks our sleep.

"Yeah," Specialist Percy Ferriss answers.

"The First Sergeant wants to see you."

"Alright, on my way," he replied followed by a few choice words of what he thought of the First Sergeant, the individual who woke him up, and why could it not wait until the morning.

"Careful with the wire," I mumbled as Ferriss crawled out the sandbag covered exit path we were sleeping in. Lucky for him he was closer to the back exit. Well, more like lucky for me in that I had no one trying to crawl over me to get out.

I had just closed my eyes and was falling back into a deep sleep when.

WHOOSH BANG!

I threw my eyes open just in time to see that all too familiar white light followed this time by complete darkness and the ringing in my ears came back with a vengeance. Then almost immediately, a very loud and deep thud caused the floor to shake. I was hit in the face by flying dirt, small debris, and dust. I do not know what overcame me but I high tailed it out the same exit that Ferriss went out just a few seconds earlier.

The ringing in my ears was still very much present but I could hear machinegun fire and people yelling "Cease Fire!"

I distinctly remember hearing someone say, "Shit, who hit another mortar round?"

What I did not know at the time was that people started gathering in front of the building we were in. They could tell that it was our defensive position that collapsed and they started digging through the fallen sandbags.

I managed to make it to the Platoon CP where the Platoon Leader, Platoon Sergeant and the LT's RTO asked me what that noise was. I looked at them stunned. I guess I was a little out of it or just could not hear what they were saying. They looked at me and repeatedly called my name. "GUERRA! WHAT HAPPENED?"

"Sir, Sergeant, our position blew up and then fell down," answering over the ringing in my ears.

"What do you mean it blew up?"

"We were asleep, then Ferriss got called out, and then I was falling asleep when the explosion happened and then the sandbag walls and cover just collapsed."

"Were you in the position when it fell?"

"No, I was in the covered exit tunnel we made. It's probably still standing."

"So are you and Ferriss OK?" Laffington yelling at me asked.

"Ferriss was not there when it went off. I just have this ringing in my ears."

Ferriss rushes into the room that serves as the Platoon CP.

"Sergeant! The First Sergeant wants everyone to help get…" stopping in mid-sentence when he looks at me.

"Help with what Specialist?"

"You are not at the bottom of the pile of sandbags?" he asks looking at me in disbelief.

"WHAT?" I respond.

"First Sergeant wanted everyone to help dig you out."

"Come On, Guerra. Let's go tell the First Sergeant you are still with us." Laffington said as he slapped me on the shoulder.

We proceeded to walk back to the front of the building. Along the way, we crossed several concertina wire obstacles.

"Specialist Guerra," Lt. Roberts said in an inquisitive tone.

"Yes, sir."

"How did you manage to make it to the CP in the dark without tripping over any of the Concertina wire?"

"Beats me, sir. I completely forgot it was there. Hey, my hearing is coming back."

Fifteen minutes later the entire company is standing in formation with the Battalion Commander talking to the company commander in front of the formation. The Company Commander was reporting to the Battalion Commander that every individual assigned to the company was either present or accounted for. Everyone was also very much alive without as much as a scratch from the collapsing defensive position.

"Alright men back to your positions. Fall out!" said the Company Commander.

"Guerra are you two going to be OK in your position? We'll fix it at first light," asked Laffington.

"What if they attack at first light?"

"Then it really will be truly a very hasty fighting position."

Once we made it back to our position. Ferriss and I started working at quickly fortifying the front of the position so that we had something to work with. Within fifteen minutes were back in the covered exit path ready to get a couple of hours of sleep. My ears had definitely stopped ringing.

"Ferriss, what did the First Sergeant want?"

"I dunno. I never made it."

"Huh?"

"I was almost at the CP when I heard the explosion."

"I turned around to see if I could see something like a flame or anything. I saw nothing. I was trying to get my bearings when he ran out the building he was in and ran into me. He asked me where the noise came from I told him the general area and we took off. By the time, we got in front of the building others were already digging out the sandbags. The first sergeant called out SSG Laffington's name and that's when he told me to go get him."

"Do you know who it was that called you out because I couldn't recognize the voice?"

"I think it was Corporal Sams," referring to the Company Clerk Corporal John Sams, "but come to think of it, it didn't really sound like Sams."

"You think it was a set up?"

"Not really, I bet someone from the OPFOR was screwing around with us. Do you remember that time in the Grunewald, when we hitched up their trailer to our deuce and a half? The trailer was packed with the hot chow mermites."

"Oh yeah, the best dinner I ever had in the field. Steaks, mashed potatoes, and gravy. Yeah, it had to be payback!" Well, that is what I wanted to think at the time. It made sense as we were always going up against each other in the training field and parade field.

"All this talk about food and the excitement tonight has got me hungry. We had better get some sleep. Oh five fifteen is gonna come sooner than you think."

"Damn straight, compadre."

CHAPTER SIXTEEN

WEST BERLIN, GERMANY • US SECTOR • PARKS RANGE • DOUGHBOY CITY • COMPANY A AREA OF OPERATIONS • OCTOBER 12, 1989 • THURSDAY • 0648HRS

After spending the night in what was left of our hasty defensive fighting position, well in the sandbag-covered tunnel, we still had guard duty to pull. Being up earlier than everyone else gave us time to fire up some heat tabs and cook up some coffee in our metal canteen cups long before chow arrived. Nothing beats hot coffee on a cold morning especially when you are the last two to pull guard duty. That's right, tenure definitely has its privileges. We had pulled many middle shifts, which are a great inconvenience, but as we started to become old timers in the platoon, Wils, Brown, Ferriss, and I still had to pull guard duty but it was either at the beginning or at the end. The middle was strictly reserved for the FNGs (Finally New Guys) and it stayed that way until there were new FNGs to take over the middle shifts.

Around 0600, we started waking up the rest of the platoon. About 45 minutes later, Sgt. Summit, SSG Williams, Ferriss and I started to work on the fallen position. As we were clearing the sandbags closest to the front window, Staff Sergeant Williams called me over.

"Yes, Sergeant Williams."

"Here you go. Put this in your trophy case," he said as he handed to me what appeared to be the bottom remnants of three artillery simulators that were taped together by hundred mile an hour tape (OD green duct tape).

"Three of them? Could they really have the power to knock it down?"

"You were there you tell me. There is no shrapnel. It had to be the overpressure as it blew to the sides. It wasn't the front because of the big

73

open window space."

"Yes, I know they make a lot of noise when they go off and I remember what Sergeant Stracklind's hand looked like after that small simulator went off while he was holding it."

"You know what Guerra?"

"What, Sergeant?"

"Between you and me, I don't think it was 4th Battalion that did this."

"What do you mean Sergeant Williams?"

"All of us heard Herndez when he came back. He was pissed about something. Whatever happened yesterday afternoon with him and the MPs it really fired him up."

"So, you think he did it?"

"Oh no, he's not that stupid. He would never do it on his own but he could talk someone in his squad into doing it because it would be fun."

"Do you think it was just someone blowing off steam?"

"Yes, just that someone did not really think things through."

"I see. Just blowing off steam," I said to myself.

"Come on, let's get things ready."

As we walked off back into the room that housed our hasty fighting position. Ferriss and Sgt. Summit had the hasty part of the defensive fighting position all done. There was not going to be time to improve and fortify the position as we did the past couple of days. It would have to do the way it was.

As Ferriss and I were finishing up quietly, I got to thinking about what Staff Sergeant Williams was saying. It was not 4th Battalion but SSG Herndez or one of his cronies. What did they say to him to set him off? Did the CID agents flat out confront him and tell him that I was the one that brought him to their attention? Does he think that I am blaming him for Vela's death or that I am accusing him of doing something with Vela's wife? Geez, there are just too many questions. It could be my imagination along with a little paranoia mixed in with the stress of lack of sleep, filling sandbags, getting my brain bucket rattled, and rebuilding the fighting position.

"Guerra!"

"Huh? Yeah?"

"Here we go! Look over by that building"

"Which one? Oh, wait the yellow smoke I see it."

More artillery simulators, smoke grenades popping, and the sounds of the M16s and M60 Machineguns firing blank ammunition followed. The long awaited attack was on. After all this time and heartache, the Opposing Force (OPFOR) was making its assault from the same hill we were going to on that foggy morning not so long ago.

It was over within 30 minutes. The assault and the ensuing

counterattack were nothing but a blur. It was always this way. We march in, fill sandbags, and use them to build these elaborate fighting positions that are far from "hasty" defensive positions then spend thirty minutes out of three days playing Good Guys versus the Bad Guys. Then what took numerous hours to put together takes only minutes to tear down.

By noon, we were packed and ready for the road march back to McNair. However, it was not until 1500 that we lined up and started the march back. The walk was uneventful and quiet. There was, however, one small incident on the way back.

A BVG bus, ever on time, refused to wait as we were trying to cross Goerzallee at Wismarer Strasse. Almost took out half the company. The look on the bus driver's face was as if he was going to wet himself when First Sergeant Kiddle walked out in front of the bus and stopped, pulled out his Colt M1911 .45 Pistol, loaded a magazine, it was an empty magazine, and pointed it at the bus. The First Sergeant stood still until the last man in Alpha Company was clear. Then the First Sergeant holstered his weapon, walked over to the driver's side of the bus, knocked on the window, when the driver opened it, he stuck his hand in the window to shake the bus driver's hand, said "Danke" and then rejoined the marching column. For as far as any of us know the bus driver is still there stunned at what had just transpired.

CHAPTER SEVENTEEN

WEST BERLIN, GERMANY • UK SECTOR •
KURFÜRSTENDAMM • JOACHIMSTALER STRASSE 15 •
KU'DORF DISCO & BAR • OCTOBER 28, 1989 •
SATURDAY • 2240HRS

Things had been quiet the past two weeks. Well, at least on this side of the wall it was somewhat quiet. Somewhat. Ann and I were at the Ku'dorf. We had been there a while when some friends showed up.

"Hey, Kids." said Melissa York, Ann's school friend, over the musical styling of Milli Vanilli's 'Girl You Know It's True' that the popular nightclub among the US and British soldiers was playing.

"Hi, here sit down next to me," said Ann.

I scooted over in the booth we were sitting at. As I settled into my new spot, I looked up at Melissa and just over her shoulder, I thought I saw a familiar face. Then I looked over at Ann, who gave me a puzzled look back. Then I looked back over Melissa's shoulder and nothing.

"What's wrong?"

"Nothing, I thought I saw someone?"

"Who?" as she looked in the direction I was looking at but saw exactly what I saw, nothing but people having a good time.

"No one. I must be tired it's been a busy week."

"You guys OK or should I leave?" asked Melissa.

"We're fine. Dan's had some problems since his friend died."

"Oh, I'm sorry."

"It's OK."

"Hey, we're here to party. So let's party," I changed the tone of the conversation.

"Yeah!" Tyler said as he and his date showed up in front of our table.

"Hey man, what are you two up to?" I said as I put a big smile on my face. I felt better having someone that I knew close by. Someone that would have my back just in case. Of course, the Ku'dorf was packed with American soldiers and they would gladly join in any fracas so long as it met the "us versus them" criteria. However, on a one-on-one situation you were on your own. Having Tyler around made me feel better in that in a one-on-one there would be no room for cheap shots from outsiders and if there were my friend would address them accordingly.

"Not much, we came in to check out what has happening. We'll be here a while. You guys wanna join us at the Irish Pub later?"

"Yes, sure." Melissa answered for us and Ann nodded in agreement.

"OK troops, we'll talk to you later." They moved out to find a place to sit of their own. Eventually, they worked through the crowd in the ring that surrounds the dance floor in the disco portion of the Ku'dorf and found a spot close to the DJ booth.

Ann, Melissa, and I drank and danced a bit. It was about 40 minutes later when Tyler and his date got up and left. We made eye contact and I waved him out. It was almost immediately after that the uneasy feeling returned. Ann must have picked up on it.

"Come on, let's dance one more time. Then we can go." She knew exactly what to say and when to say it, Ann is definitely a keeper.

"OK."

"Hey, where you going?" asked Melissa.

"We're gonna dance." Ann replied.

We made our way to the dance floor, as we got ready to dance the song came to an end. I guess the DJ had his attention elsewhere because there was that dreaded silent pause. Then a familiar guitar lick starts coming across the speakers and the crowd rushes the dance floor. 'GO! GO! Go with a smile...' and the title song from one of the most popular movies of the year starts to play.

The crowd on that small dance floor really made any kind of dancing almost impossible. It was just a lot of swaying and little hip shaking. Then the crowd grew tighter, it was as if all the other bars in the Ku'dorf emptied into the dance floor. Then, to top it off, Melissa started dancing with us. Don't get me wrong, I like Melissa a lot but sometimes she can be at the wrong place at the wrong time. Ann noticed her and started dancing with her and in the moment she looked away, a couple of people danced between us.

"Specialist Guerra," a familiar unfamiliar voice whispered in my ear.

"What?" I said as I turned to face who called my name. It was the first watch guy from the Kaufhof store in East Berlin. "What the fu...."

"Sssh. Please do not say anything," he said as he leaned in so that I could hear him.

"Who the fuck are you?"

"Please, Herr Guerra. We don't have much time."

"We?" Just then, I noticed who was dancing between Ann and me. It was his partner, the other watch guy from the vodka store. He put his right index finger to his mouth making the "be quiet" hand signal. I quickly got the idea they were ready to make their move.

"We know who did it. We want to help you…"

"HEY!!! HALT!!! GET HIM!!!" someone in the far corner of the disco called out. I turned to look at who was actually louder than the song. He looked like an American pointing at me and the guy next to me. By the time I turned to look at the first watch guy, they were both gone into the crowd.

The American made his way to me and hustled me off the dance floor and to the first bar immediately to the left after leaving the disco.

"Master Sergeant William Raynes, I'm with the 766th. We've been following you for some time now."

"Yeah, I had a feeling."

"A feeling? Did one of us say something to you?"

"Sergeant, every once in a while I would get this feeling that I was being watched."

"OK, look what did that guy say to you?"

"All he said was that they know who did it and that they want to help?"

"Did what?"

"I don't know what he's talking about."

Putting his left index finger up to his left ear, "OK, don't worry we'll get them later, out."

I looked at him with a puzzled look on my face.

"Yes, Specialist? Oh, they seem to have disappeared. We had someone outside and they split up."

"You should know these are the same two guys from East Berlin."

"Let's move up front."

We moved to the top of the stairwell that acts as the entrance to the Ku'dorf. At this time of night, there is no one in line to get in so we could talk.

"You mean these are the same two individuals you and your squad ran into in East Berlin?"

"Yes, Sergeant."

"Crap. Follow me."

We walked over to a taxi that was parked around the corner on Lietzenburger Strasse. Actually, the car was a BMW Taxi that had a few enhancements added from what I could see, there were probably more. The three two-way radios under the dash were a big giveaway. One thing was certain, whoever drove this car was not using the three radios to listen to AFN-Berlin (the Armed Forces Network radio station based in Berlin).

MSG Raynes of the 766th Military Intelligence Detachment told me to stay put.

"Oh shit, Ann!" I forgot that I walked out of the Ku'dorf without so much as telling her I was leaving. I would not blame her if she went home. However, I did not want to chance it.

Tapping on the car window Raynes looks up while talking into one of the handheld microphones.

"My girlfriend, she doesn't know I'm here"

Lowering the window just enough for me to hear, "Specialist Guerra, I am giving you a direct order you will stay here until I say you can leave."

"Yes, Sergeant."

A minute or so later, he exits his vehicle.

"Specialist, I just got off the radio with CID. They want you to stop by their office. However, they will call you when they can talk to you. Seems that this is the busy season for CID."

"OK, he's on his way," putting his left index finger up to his left ear.

"Look, as a courtesy we'll let you continue with your evening. These guys have been burned and they more than likely won't make contact with you again. Well, at least not tonight. Now, you can head on back to the Ku'dorf. Your girlfriend and her friend are still inside but at the coat check. If you hurry you should meet her at the top of the stairs."

"OK, Thanks Sarge." I was shocked and just in awe at how much these guys knew.

I made it back to the Ku'dorf in time to catch up with Ann and Melissa. We headed over to the Irish Pub at the bottom of the Europa Center. That place was also packed. Luckily, Tyler and his date were still there. They had a table in the back. We joined them. That's when Ann asked me what happened.

"Some guys started hassling me."

"Who was that guy that called out? MP?"

"I don't know, he was American. He tried to help me catch them but they got away."

"What did they say?" asked Tyler.

"I couldn't make it out the music was a little too loud. It sounded like they said they knew who did it and they could help me." I said leaning in so that not everyone could hear.

"Did what?"

"Yeah, that's what I'd like to know."

"Are they here now? We can get them and hold them for the MPs?"

"Nah, they ran off. The guy that helped me go after them, I think, was an MP"

"You think?"

"When we got to the street outside the Ku'dorf, they were gone and he said something about we'll get them later."

"Dan, what do you want to drink?" Ann called out as she made a motion to the waitress standing there to take our order.

"Jack and Coke please. Double Jack."

We spent the next hour there with our drinks and listening to some Irish band that was in from County Cork playing some nice tunes. It was time to leave as Ann had a commitment with her parents in the morning and it was time to bring this exciting evening to a close.

CHAPTER EIGHTEEN

WEST BERLIN, GERMANY • US SECTOR • McNAIR BARRACKS • 6th BATTALION 502nd INFANTRY AREA • DINING FACILITY • NOVEMBER 2, 1989 • THURSDAY • 0750HRS

For the most part, it was business as usual at McNair. The DDR, on the other hand, was still dealing with its citizens demanding reforms and the government appeared to be going through the motions with them. Things have really started to heat up for them. It seems that the East German government has been trying to negotiate with the "NEW FORUM" group, which claims to have a membership of just under 30,000 people, making it the largest opposition group in East Germany. The New Forum Group wanted real reforms put in place and changes made now, not later.

As for us, on this side of the wall, not since we were there three weeks ago, has anyone been back to Doughboy. The word was that the East Germans through the Soviets through "unofficial" channels were worried that our conducting training so close to the East German frontier that "certain groups" might use our presence in the area as an opportunity for members of those groups to head to West Berlin. Therefore, to put at ease any tensions, the Command declared that we were not going to give the East Germans any more problems. They had enough on their plate. Yeah, well who does not have more than enough on their plate, right now?

Speaking of plates, I was in line for morning chow. The line had pretty much thinned out by the time I arrived. Ferriss, Brown, and Wils were inside eating their breakfast. In front of me, were a few people from 1st and 2nd Platoon as well as several others from the other companies in the battalion.

As I was waiting at the back of the line, someone decided to push in the back of my knees causing my legs to buckle and I fell straight to the floor. As soon as I could turn to see who did it, I see a smile go on the face of Staff Sergeant Herndez.

"Hey, Sergeant that's not cool."

"At ease, Specialist," he looks around at others in the line in front of me looking back to see what the commotion is all about.

I start to get up when he grabs my left arm first from under my left shoulder then he wraps his other arm around me. Not wanting to be seen, he pulls my left arm behind my back.

"Here. Let me help you up, Specialist."

I verbally let him and everyone around know that whatever he was doing hurt. So what does he do? He puts a little more upward force adding to the discomfort.

"Let's go to the Infirmary. I got you. I hope you didn't break your arm when you fell."

"Sergeant why are you doing this?" I asked.

"Cállate pendejo," he led me down the hall to the stairwell. Where he slammed me against the railing.

"What the fuck is your problem?" the only words that I felt were worthy of saying to him came out.

"I told you to shut the fuck up, pendejo!"

I just stood there looking at him. He had fire in his eyes and he was out for blood. He was beyond pissed and this was not going to end well for either one of us.

He stepped up to me and leaned in, "You think you are so very smart Specialist Guerra?"

"What are you talking about Sergeant?"

After a quick and unexpected jab to my gut, he leans over and says, "You don't know shit, hermano. You don't know what is going on. I suggest you keep your mouth shut if you know what's good for you. Mi entiendes? You understand? ¡Cállate la boca!"

"Sergeant, I really don't know what you are talking about."

He looks around to see if anyone is around.

"Mire, look, it's like this. You and your Germans friends don't know who did what and right here right now they can't help you. You got that? You don't know shit."

Tyler's name flashed in my mind. Then again, they are in the same platoon. More than likely, he was talking about the weekend on the Ku'damm and what went down. Of course, Herndez being Herndez, he wanted to hear the details.

"Sergeant…" I was stopped from talking as he got closer and jammed his left forearm across my throat.

"I told you to shut up, Specialist. Man this is going to be fun. Then later you know what else is going to be fun?"

I really could not say much.

"Tu mamacita, Ann."

That did it, he just crossed that line. I tried to throw a punch.

"There you go Private. You go ahead and hit me. They will put you away and she will be mine. Give me time and eventually todas son míos."

What did he mean by eventually they are all his? A door closed at the top of the stairwell causing Herndez to step back. Immediately, I started to work my throat, trying to clear my throat and searching for a way out of there.

"Not so fast Specialist. I'm not done with you."

"Oh, I think you are now," SSG Williams pushed Herndez away from me. Unfortunately, as he came around the corner from the mess hall he saw me trying to get away. The door upstairs was perfect timing.

"Staff Sergeant Williams, I am pressing charges against this Specialist. He assaulted me."

"OK, come on let's go call the MPs."

Herndez steps back, obviously not expecting SSG Williams' response.

"Sergeant Williams, can I talk to you?"

"No! Are we calling the MPs or not?" asks Williams.

"Fuck you Specialist, I am not done with you." Herndez turns and walks away. He makes certain to flip me the bird before he gets to top of the first landing of the stairway.

"Thank you, Sergeant Williams."

"Are you ok?"

"Yes, that guy has lost his mind."

"Remember what I told you out at Doughboy?"

"Yes, Sergeant."

"I recommend for the time being you don't do anything by yourself."

"I will try."

"Have you eaten?"

"No, I was in line when he came up behind me."

There was noise coming from the stairwell and the down the hall from the mess hall.

"Come on, let's go eat and you can tell me what just happened."

CHAPTER NINETEEN

WEST BERLIN, GERMANY • US SECTOR • ANDREWS BARRACKS • CID INTERROGATION ROOM A • NOVEMBER 9, 1989 • THURSDAY • 1700HRS

"That's it!" I got up from my chair.

"Specialist, like I told you it is going to be your word versus his word."

"Are you certain Staff Sergeant," Emmett looks down at the notes he took, "Williams didn't see or hear something more?"

"No, he would have said or done something more."

"Very well. I am going to be very blunt with you Specialist. This does not look good."

"Good, is that enough to get him?"

"No, I think you misunderstood me. It does not look good for you."

"Me? What did I do?"

"It's real simple. You don't have any proof. You have all but confessed to actively communicating with the enemy."

"They approached me. I didn't go to them."

"Yes, but you made no attempt to apprehend them as the MI Agent told you to apprehend them."

"Whoa, first off, I did not know what was going on until that Master Sergeant told me what was happening."

"That's not the way the Court Martial board will see it."

"Court Martial?"

"Yes, if you keep this up, Staff Sergeant Herndez is going to come gunning for you. We will be required to report this entire conversation."

"But…" I decided I already said too much.

"No buts, if he wants to he can have you brought up on charges."

I just nodded my head in agreement.

"Listen, go back to your unit and stick close to someone. If the Staff Sergeant tries anything there will be a witness."

"A witness, is that all I need?"

"Yes, someone to corroborate your story. You know this."

"So all I need is someone to see him do something wrong and then you can arrest him?"

"Well, it's not as simple as that. There has to be indisputable proof. There also has to be no signs that he was setup or fraud was committed just to catch him."

Again nodding my head.

"Look don't go and do something stupid just to prove your point," spoke Agent Walter.

"Exactly! Let me tell you something that is very, very true. In all our years of police work, criminals will always do something stupid. They always give themselves away. Therefore, if what you believe to be true is true it is just a matter of time until he tips his hat. Let's just hope you are not the one that happens to be the last one to cross his path," said Agent Emmett.

"I understand."

"Don't just understand but know that if you do something to provoke him or put him in a situation that backs him into a corner or that he has to defend himself you will be the one back in this room, this time in cuffs."

"I won't mess with him, I promise Agent."

"See to it," said Agent Walter.

"OK Guerra, go back to your unit and lay low."

We start walking out of the interrogation room and into a common area, which has several desks chairs, a wall locker, and several secure cage doors. There are a few people gathered at the far end of the room by some two-way radio units and a couple of television sets.

"Can I go get a Döner before I go back to McNair?"

"Do whatever you want just stay away from you know who," said Agent Emmett.

Just as I start heading to the front door, someone from the group huddled around the radios and TVs turns around and calls to Special Agent Emmett.

"What's the matter?"

"Come over here and check this out!" moving his head to refer to whatever was happening on the TVs or coming across the radios.

"Alright, give me second."

Turning his attention back to me.

"Alright Specialist. Take it easy. This is not over, not by a long shot. Just don't make the situation any worse than it is."

"OK, thank you, Agent Emmett," I said as I started my way out of the building and to Al's across the street from Andrew's Barracks. Al Molino's was a small restaurant and bar frequented mostly by the members of the Berlin Brigade that lived across the street. Al's has one of the best Döner Kebab's in Berlin. The Döner Kebab is a Turkish dish made with meat cooked on a vertical spit, normally lamb meat is used but also a mixture of veal or beef, or sometimes chicken. Along with the meat is included a salad consisting of chopped lettuce, cabbage, onions, cucumber, and tomatoes, as well as a yogurt sauce. The filling is served in a thick flatbread that is usually toasted or warmed. I purchased two. I always buy two, one for now and one for a snack later tonight with a few Michelob's makes watching whatever is on AFN-Berlin bearable.

I walked back inside the gate of Andrews to wait for the West Bus back to McNair. I could take the East bus for a nice leisurely return to McNair but there was a buzz in the air and I felt something inside telling me to get back to McNair as soon as I could. The East or West Bus was an internal bus route that ran either clockwise or counter-clockwise around the major US military installations and housing areas in the American Sector of Berlin. It was based out of the Transportation Motor Pool at Andrews. The US Military members, their family members, contractors and LS/LN personnel of the Berlin Command used the free bus service. It was a way to travel to and from the PX and Commissary at Truman Plaza, across the street from Clay Headquarters Compound, without having to use and pay to ride on the Berlin BVG bus and subway system.

It was about 1820hrs, when the West bus made the right turn at the front gate of McNair Barracks from Goerzallee. We were delayed as there were several green army buses, a hand full of deuce and a half trucks, and numerous Humvees preparing to move out of McNair. They all had their yellow warning lights flashing on top of each vehicle. Something was going on but the configuration was all wrong for an Alert. Usually, the buses would meet us at the end of the road march and not take us out. The soldiers that I did see were not moving with any sense of urgency but there was a sense of urgency about the whole thing. Then again, I was inside the bus and only managed to pick up what I could when the bus driver, an LS Contractor, and the LN Guard of the 6941st Guards Battalion had an excited exchange about the "Ossis" and someone named Schabowski and a press conference.

CHAPTER TWENTY

WEST BERLIN, GERMANY • US SECTOR • McNAIR BARRACKS • 6th BATTALION 502nd INFANTRY AREA • COMPANY A • 3rd PLATOON LIVING AREA • NOVEMBER 9, 1989 • THURSDAY • 1930HRS

I had finished the first of three Michelob beers that were in the room's mini-fridge as I was watching Batman on the VCR. Ann's family purchased a copy last month and this was the first chance I had to watch this movie. I was really looking forward to it.

"Hey, I was just checking my mail box and Garon was telling the CQ that the East Germans are going to let people come across," said Ferriss.

"What are you talking about?" hitting the pause button on the VCR remote control.

"Garon was telling Sgt. Meadows that his girlfriend called him to find out if we were going on alert. He asked what she was talking about and she said that it was all on TV. The news said that the East Germans had a meeting and decided to allow East Germans to travel to the west. That there was a news conference and that the border was open right now."

"Wow! You know what this means?"

"Yeah, the Russians are coming!"

"This is huge. If they are really opening the border there is going to be chaos. Did Garon say anything else?"

"No, just that he was going down to Checkpoint Charlie, seems that's where people are supposed to come across first."

"Well, I highly doubt they'll walk to no-man's land and cross the mine fields and tank traps to hop over the wall."

"Do you want to go?"

"Man, I am watching Batman. Besides they said I should stay close to home."

"They also said that if you go out you gotta go with others. Well, I'm going and once I'm gone you can't go by yourself," said Ferriss.

"I know...OK," looking over at the two empty sleeping areas in our shared room, "What about Brown? Where is he?"

"Last time I saw him, he was heading upstairs."

"Guess he won't be joining us." I said as I was realizing just how much time Brown was spending with the non-11Bravos from Headquarters Company. I was starting to wonder what he was up to with them.

"So we going?" asked Ferriss.

"You better believe it. How many times do we get to experience history? I mean if this is real then this is going to be the greatest single event in our entire lives. If it turns out the be the prelude to war then this is definitely going to be the greatest single event of our very short lives."

About 20 minutes later, we were on the 10 bus North to Oskar-Helene Heim. Then on the U2 to Wittenbergplatz where we changed trains to the U3 line and on to Hallesches Tor where we changed trains again. This time it was on to the U6 north to Kochstrasse exiting just feet from Checkpoint Charlie.

As we exited the subway station, there was definitely something going on. There was a crowd on both sides of the wall. From the top of the steps of the subway station exit, we could see people gather from here to Checkpoint Charlie and on the far side we could make out a line of headlights, obviously Trabants. Through the beams of yellow lights, Ferriss and I could most definitely make out people on the other side of the East Berlin processing center. There were so many people crammed in this small area, the last time I saw this many people gathered at one spot was at the Pink Floyd concert back on June 6 in front of the Reichstag.

There were television crews running around trying to set up to get that perfect shot. This street is so narrow that either the perfect shot unfortunately will be from the middle of the street or somewhere out there on the death strip among the landmines and the dog runs. I wonder if the East Germans would let them cross over for that perfect shot?

At the southwest corner of Kochstrasse and Friedrichstrasse, we saw an MP standing outside his Humvee, which was parked on the corner, literally all four wheels on the sidewalk. He was talking to someone in Army Class A's as we walked over to talk to the MP. As we got closer, we could hear the conversation.

"Yeah, it's a freaking zoo over there," said the Staff Sergeant carrying a small backpack, which we typically used to carry back over two or three bottles of Stolichnaya and one bag from the Kaufhof.

"Did they give you any hassle when you were coming across?" asked the MP.

"No, they were more worried about the East Berliners than they were about the Americans. Yeah, the Russians moved me along as if they didn't want me to stop for any reason. They all had a worried look on their faces. I just got an uneasy feeling when I saw the same look on the faces of the East German Border Guards."

"What do you mean?"

"It was like they did not want to be there when the shit hit the fan. You know it's like you know there is going to be a car crash and you are in the back seat, you can't do anything to prevent the crash and you can't get out. That's the look the Russians, all of them, had and the feeling I got was that they really wanted to jump out of that speeding car."

"So do you think it's going to get ugly?"

"Look Sergeant, if it gets ugly there is nothing we can do about it and from what I saw, there is nothing the Russians can do about it as well. The VOPOs and Border Guards are just as confused as the rest of us, only problem is that they have standing orders to shoot to kill."

"Guess we'll just have to wait and see," said the MP who then looked over at us and said, "You guys aren't planning on sticking around?"

"We just came to see if it was true."

"Well I suggest you two stick close by especially if we have to didi mau in a hurry."

"We were planning to walk over to Zimmerstasse by the checkpoint." I told him what we had planned on doing.

"If the shit hits the fan like the Sergeant said then I am leaving this position and falling back to Mehringplatz about five or six blocks south of here. In the meantime, I have to monitor traffic flow until the Polizei arrive which should be any minute now. So don't get in anyone's way and be sure to get out of the way the moment any crazy shit starts to happen," and with that the MP secured his Humvee and moved out to the middle of street and tried to keep traffic moving.

We moved out heading north into the sea of humanity and to the very tip of the Cold War spear, again.

CHAPTER TWENTY-ONE

WEST BERLIN, GERMANY • US SECTOR • CHECKPOINT CHARLIE • NOVEMBER 9, 1989 • THURSDAY • 2240HRS

We made it to Zimmerstrasse, the street that paralleled the Berlin Wall from Checkpoint Charlie back to Potsdamer Platz where the wall turned north towards the Brandenburg Gate and the Reichstag. It was fantastic being around all this energy of the people. There certainly was an air of hopefulness and uncertainty shared by everyone tonight. There was also a sense of danger in that if something did go horribly wrong tonight, the ensuing stampede would not be a good thing. If there were a thousand people at Checkpoint Charlie tonight, I know I would be counting too low. I just cannot get over how many people are here.

Throughout the evening, we ran across other Americans, British, and French soldiers and their family members. Mostly, it was West Berliners enjoying this moment in time. Another history in the making moment in Berlin. This city was full of historical moments.

From the nonsense of Hitler and his crew, the Soviets and the Battle for Berlin, the month long occupation of the Soviets before the US & UK took their place in West Berlin, the Berlin Blockade and the subsequent Airlift, the 17 June 1956 uprising in East Berlin, the construction of the Berlin Wall, the numerous successful escapes, and the high profile deaths at the wall. None was as high profile as that of Peter Fechter who was shot by the East Germans and left to die just feet from freedom and medical attention. One cannot come to this city and not be affected by all the tragedy that has happened because of this wall and this division of people. Tonight things were different.

As the evening wore on the mood started to change. It started to turn into a party mood. Plenty of drinking, singing, and chanting. At one point, Ferriss and I both swore that the East Berliners were chanting right along with the West Berliners. Then it happened. There was cheering from the East.

At 10:45pm, 9 November 1989, the first Trabant left the East German Control Point and drove down the small winding road that was Friedrichstrasse, at this point, and straight through Checkpoint Charlie. The MP just waved the car through. Then more cars and more cheering. A couple of minutes later the first of the large pedestrian traffic started coming through from the East. The West Berliners kicked the party into high gear. More Beer, Champagne, more cheers, more tears of joy, and a lot of hugging and kissing. For this moment, the whole world came to a halt. As soon as that first Trabant came across the Cold War started to thaw. We joined in the ensuing celebration.

From our spot on Zimmerstrasse, we could see the television reporters and their camera crews rushing the people that were coming across. By now, the MPs at Checkpoint Charlie were worried that those driving into West Berlin would run over those that were walking into West Berlin. They were no longer maintaining the building that processed the Allies when they moved to and from East Berlin instead they were outside working the crowd. Traffic was starting to back up and that was not acceptable. A couple of Trabants broke down at the intersection of Kochstrasse and Friedrichstrasse. Good thing the Berlin Polizei was here making sure things did not get out of hand. However, all of them were being stretched thin.

From what we could pick up from the crowd, it seems that starting at the Bornholmer Strasse checkpoint then followed by all the access points in and out of Berlin, they all opened at approximately the same time and there were traffic jams at all crossing points. If the Warsaw Pact wanted to do something, I would say give it another thirty minutes and the time would be right for them to act. At this point, everyone here was not going anywhere fast.

"Come on! Let's move to get a better view." I told Ferriss who was in complete agreement.

Over the course of the next five minutes, we moved a total of 50 feet. It was that bad, that crowded. We were now on the path the East Berliners were taking as they walked past Checkpoint Charlie.

Through the crowd a hand reached over and grabbed the right shoulder of my coat, I turned to see who it was.

"I told you, I wasn't done with you, pendejo," it was Staff Sergeant Herndez.

I never saw the gravity knife come out of his pocket but that unique click the blade makes after releasing it and snapping into place by the holder's unique flick of the wrist. That click might as well have been playing over the Polizei loud speaker it was just that loud.

Being ahead of me by a few steps Ferriss never knew that Herndez was here. I had no time to get his attention in the loud crowd. It was then that Herndez made his move. As he started to go for my gut with the gravity knife, I spun away to the left and out of my black Member's Only jacket. That was good for me but I took SSG Herndez by surprise and he kept moving with his blade until it stopped.

It stopped only after it entered the chest of an East German that had just taken his first few steps of freedom. As I started making my quick getaway across Friedrichstrasse, I was almost hit by a driver of a Trabant who showed no signs of stopping.

There was a scream from a woman who saw Herndez holding the blade in his hand. She also saw the blood of the young East Berliner pour out of his chest and then fall to the floor. Then more screams. This snapped Herndez out of whatever daze he was in. He threw the jacket he was holding in his left hand on top of the person he had just stabbed. Looking for me, he saw me trying to make my way across the street, and took off after me.

Later, I found out that Ferriss had turned around to see where the screams were coming from and saw the crowd make an opening around the young man on the floor. He saw my jacket and blood spilling out from underneath it.

"Oh shit. Guerra!" he pushed his way through the two or three people between him and the body.

As he kneeled down over the body he began to take the jacket off the body, the screaming continued and the calls for the Polizei began. Ferris removed the jacket only to see that it was not my face but rather it was a blonde-haired, blue-eyed male with a puzzled look on his face. The young man was starting to go into shock. Ferriss' skills kicked in and he started applying pressure to the wound or what he thought was the wound as it was where the blood was coming from. He started calling out, "MPs HELP! Man DOWN! MEDIC! HELP POLIZEI!"

At that same moment, I could hear someone yell, "HALT!"

I looked back only to see a crowd of people yelling behind me. I was already past the Checkpoint Charlie Museum and behind me, I could see someone holding a knife over his head as he made his way through the crowd. It had to be Herndez. He was getting closer. For a second, all I thought about was how people would not move even when I would politely excuse myself but have someone hold a knife over his head and suddenly a path is created. People.

In the second or two, that I used to catch my breath Herndez was now a few feet behind me.

"You better stop, Specialist, that's an order." He yelled out.

"HALT! oder ich schieße" someone behind him yelled again.

I started moving through the crowd and this time I was taking no prisoners. I was just a few feet from Kochstrasse. The only problem was that I was on the wrong corner of the intersection. I still had to get across Kochstrasse and then Friedrichstrasse. Yes, that had to be the path to take. If I could lose him even just for a second in front of the stairs down to the Kochstrasse U-bahn station, he might think I went down the stairs. I could make it to the Humvee and the MP.

I took my first step onto Kochstrasse and from out of nowhere, another Trabant almost hit me. I looked right in the eye of the driver then I saw a woman and few kids in the back seat. I actually yelled, "Entschuldigen Sie!" and hopped over the hood. I hope it bought me a few seconds because I could actually feel the vehicle lunge forward as I was making my way across the top. I had my right hand firmly planted on the hood and when I landed, I was turned around by the forward momentum of the vehicle and it moved my arm out from underneath me. It was not that bad, I was still on my feet. I did see Herndez fighting to get across but his eyes fixed right on me.

Now why did he not have the same luck with Trabants that I did or at least with a fast moving BVG bus?

"HALT!!! für verdammte Scheiße halt!" that was the Polizei behind us somewhere. I made it to the southeastern corner of Kochstrasse and Friedrichstrasse. I could stop but I knew that Herndez would get to me long before the men in green would even get anywhere close to stopping him. No time to eye the street, I started crossing Friedrichstrasse. I had never hoped for a crowd of people to enter the subway as I did at that moment. I guess some things are never meant to be.

As I crossed in front of the stairwell there was no one coming from Checkpoint Charlie. I saw no one walking in this direction. In a sea of humanity, I happen to pick the only deserted island. Well, I had to keep going as the MP Humvee was just on the other side of the street or was it? I did not see the blue flashing light. All the other vehicles had their lights on. No blue flashing light.

Crap, I knew that I was not going to make it to Mehringdamm without him catching me. Just then, another Trabant slammed on his breaks right in front of me.

"GET IN!!!" wait a second; I know this face and voice. "GET IN NOW!" the back door opens. I get in.

As the door shuts, I look back to see Herndez stopped at the top of the stairs only long enough to get tackled down that same flight of stairs by at least two Berlin Polizei.

"Specialist Guerra, allow me to introduce myself. I am Lieutenant Konstantin Yushkevich and he is Ivan Timoshenko. Sitting next to you is Major General Anatoly Prevelov. He is why we are here and why we have been trying to talk to you."

The General extends his hand. I shake it. He says something in Russian.

"Da, general, my rasskazhem yemu," responds Yushkevich.

I look back at the General who makes a hand gesture wanting me to look back a Yushkevich.

"Look, I can't be in the vehicle with you. I will get in a lot of trouble. Please let me out or use your radio to call the MPs but please stop," I said.

"Yes, we will. Just not here. We must go," he answered.

"Go? Go where?"

Two Berlin Polizei and an MP Humvee lit up the night with their blue lights. Yeah, a little late boys. They were right behind us and closing.

"Pereyti bystreye!" Yushkevich says.

"Da," was Timoshenko's response as I feel the vehicle speed up. He starts to weave in and out of traffic.

"Pereyti bystreye! no ne ubit' nas!"

"Da!"

I look for a seatbelt but I do not see one back here where I am sitting. The sirens are getting louder and closer.

"Tovarishch leytenant Timoshenko yavlyayetsya khoroshim voditelem avtomobil" says the General, as he looks over at me and smiles.

"He says do not worry, Comrade Lieutenant Timoshenko is a good driver."

"Oh I'm not worried. At this speed death will come quick," I respond.

"YA ne volnovalsya. Na takoy skorosti smerti pridet bystro." Obviously translating to the General.

They look at me, start laughing and the General says "Da!"

"Where are we going? And why are you not stopping?"

"We are going to see some old friends, we will be there soon."

CHAPTER TWENTY-TWO

WEST BERLIN, GERMANY • US SECTOR • PARKS RANGE • MAIN GATE • NOVEMBER 9, 1989 • THURSDAY • 2325HRS

There turned out to be Doughboy City. When we got to the Park Range main gate at Osdorfer Strasse, waiting for us were CID Agents Walter and Emmett along with the Master Sergeant from the 766th, and another Soviet General and two more Soviet lieutenants.

Agent Emmett opened the door when we finally came to a stop. It took a second or two to realize that we had stopped. Agent Walter walked over to talk to the Polizei.

"We must see the young soldier. He is a witness to a terrible crime," said the older moustached Berlin Polizei.

"Right now, he is under United States custody and will remain that way until this matter is resolved," said Agent Walter showing the Police Officer his badge and credentials.

"You do not understand we believe he is involved in the stabbing of an East German citizen."

"No! You do not understand. He is under United States military custody and that is where he will remain. Sergeant please explain to this officer how things work in Berlin," Agent Walter spoke to the MP that was standing behind the Polizei.

"Agent, I tried telling them that but they are quite adamant."

"OK, please see if they can get someone who knows what they are doing to straighten these two out. You know what, better still, put in a call and see if Berlin Polizei Liaison Officer Reinhard is on duty. He will fix their malfunction, ASAP!"

"Yes, I will get Reinhard on the horn."

"See if you can get him out here and in the meantime," turning his attention the Polizei, "he will remain in my custody and will not leave my sight. You have my word."

"But Agent…" the Berlin Police Officer tried to say more.

"Special Agent Walter!"

"Yes, excuse me, Special Agent Walter we do not want trouble but…"

"But nothing, he stays with me and when we are done here you get him. Right now, gentlemen, I have this very urgent matter to attend. Sergeant! Make sure they stay right here."

Still on the radio, the MP acknowledges the Agent who turns and walks back to where we are standing.

"OK, Generals let's go," said Agent Emmett to the Soviet officers.

"Guerra you are with us," the Military Intelligence staff officer said. I got into the Humvee with them and the Soviets rode in the vehicle that the Soviet General rode in. We drove behind the newer buildings of Doughboy City East and stopped.

After turning on our flashlights, Lt. Yushkevich came up to me and introduced me to Major General Yuri Baseliv. We started walking to the west behind the Doughboy City complex. Yushkevich translated as Generals Baseliv and Prevelov then proceeded to tell us about how the Generals were young privates during in the Great Patriotic War. How they helped capture Berlin. They also went on to explain that before crossing the Teltow Canal their unit had stopped here, proceeded to reload on ammunition, and moved forward to provide covering fire as the great Soviet forces crossed the canal.

After the surrender of Germany, many privates were tasked to retrace their path to the city and collect or dispose of any ammunition that was left behind.

"We knew we left behind plenty of 50 millimeter mortar rounds and we did not want the rebel Germans to use them against us. However, as we finally made our way back we only seem to have collected very little of what we knew we left behind. Fearing the worst we were afraid to tell our superiors."

We walked a bit further when General Basilev asked one of the Lieutenants that was following to bring him his bag. Inside, he pulled out an old map and referred to it. They walked until they came to a spot on the hill that had a large rock sticking out of it. Then the General pulled out a very old compass, got his bearing and walked the necessary number of steps.

"Zdes'," saying after referring to the map one more time.

"The General says here?"

"Here what? All there is a bald patch of ground," said Agent Emmett.

"Leytenant kopat' zdes'"

"The General wants us to dig here."

They started digging. Carefully. Even though it was not a difficult dig as the dirt had been recently turned over they were careful. Then about a foot down, they reached what they were looking for. There, in the ground were several very rusty mortar and rocket rounds. Then the Generals started talking again.

"The General says that after they realized that the Germans were collecting the ammunition they continued moving in this direction. When they got here, they saw several old German men digging a large hole. They say that the men spoke only German so they could not talk to them. However, the Generals saw what they were doing. They had dug a hole about 6 meters in diameter and 3 meter deep. Then they buried all the ammunition they could find. Yes, from there to Teltower Canal the old farmers did our work."

Then handing over the map to the Military Intelligence sergeant, General Baseliv continued.

"The General says he could not turn over the map because things were different then. However, when we saw what your soldier did tonight Anatoly and I knew we had to do something. We also saw how dedicated this young soldier is to his friend. All the others looked bothered by the murder but this young soldier showed great concern about his dead friend. We also knew that if we did not try to tell you that this was here, that man would have an endless supply of weapons that could be easily dismissed and he could kill with such impunity and that we could not tolerate."

"OK, I understand but how did you see all this?"

"The General says he can tell you but you will not believe this story but you have to trust him."

"Trust him? After everything that has happened in this city tonight I do not know if I can trust my own eyes anymore."

The Soviets went on to explain that after the war they stayed in the military and were promoted to officers in the Artillery corps. They also stayed in Germany. While in Germany, they became actively involved in the new Artillery research and development program. They were assigned to test a new range and target designator but could not get accurate results against their adversaries along the East German – West German frontier because of the 1 km zone that kept the western forces from the frontier. However, as Berlin was unique, they requested to field test the device here. Upon approval, the device was installed in the closest tower to Doughboy City and the field test work began.

"Everything was working very well. We were getting very good readings. That is until one night we picked up unusual movement signals. We activated the device and saw the older soldier. The one this young man was running from tonight. He was carefully digging. We were able to record everything he did that night. We saw him remove the mortar rounds we saw him wrap the rounds with bandages and place it hidden. Over there," pointing to the wooded area close to where Vela died.

"They saw the older soldier?" asked Special Agent Emmett.

"Yes, the General says we saw his name tape. We also saw him that morning through the fog go back to where he hid the mortar rounds and place them in a shallow hole he had dug. We also saw him argue with the soldier that died. We saw him walk the soldier and point exactly where the dead soldier was to dig."

"You saw all of this through the fog? It was very thick that morning."

"Yes, it was a strain but our system saw it all. We also saw Guerra looking around maybe he was hearing the conversation. Then we were all but certain that the optics had been destroyed when the explosion occurred. However, we did record how the older soldier ran behind some sandbags. He positioned himself so that they were between him and the explosion."

"You say you recorded this?"

"Yes, everything that happened before, during, and after."

"Can we have a copy of this recording?"

"Here is where you must trust us. The entire project is classified. We know it exists because we have been rotating in and out of that tower since the project started but all we know is what we saw but cannot give you the proof that we know you need."

"Why tell us this now?"

"Because, soon our time here in Germany will come to an end and the allies must do everything to not let the same mistakes happen that happened forty-five years ago."

"We appreciate you telling us this and sharing the map. However, this does not prove that a murder was committed. I certainly cannot go tell the commanding general that the Soviets say it was a murder and for us to trust them."

"General Baseliv says he understands and regrets that he could not give you more than what he knows, what we all know, to be true."

"Thank you, maybe we should be getting back."

"Da!"

Just as we arrive at the vehicles one of the Generals shines a light in my face and says, "Spetsialist Daniel Guerra Tekhasskogo Amerike, vy khoroshiy soldat i vashi druz'ya dolzhny byt' vypolneny, chtoby kto-to, kak vy smotrite na nikh."

I look at Lt. Yushkevich.

"Both Generals say, 'Specialist Daniel Guerra of Texas America, you are a good soldier and your friends should be honored to have someone like you look out for them.'"

"Thank you sir," I said as I saluted both Generals.

Just as we start to get into the vehicle, the MP that was supposed to be guarding the front gate from anyone entering the grounds pulls up in his assigned Humvee. He parks facing the driver door of our Humvee.

"Agents Walter and Emmett, the Polizei asked me to tell you that they have another soldier in custody. They have Staff Sergeant Rafael Herndez in custody. They are accusing him of stabbing an East German at Checkpoint Charlie. They say they chased him and caught up to him as he was just about to go into a U-bahn station."

"What polizei station are they at?"

"Right now, the Polizei and SSG Herndez are at Krankenhaus Steglitz. Herndez is getting a cast put on his left leg. They say he broke his leg as he was trying to get away."

"Do they still need him?" referring to me.

"Yes, apparently the witnesses say that Herndez had Guerra by the coat and that he got out just as Herndez was trying to stab him and that's when he got the East German."

Looking into the Humvee, he says to me, "I hope you didn't antagonize him."

"No way, Agent. Ferriss and I were there early we even spoke to the MP and a Staff Sergeant that were talking about the mood of the East Germans before the Staff Sergeant left East Berlin."

"We'll see."

"Besides, I was trying to get away from him when those Russians picked me up."

"You know what?"

"What?"

"Someone might just believe you this time."

"Yeah, with all those witnesses who wouldn't believe me?"

EPILOGUE

After finding Staff Sergeant Herndez guilty of attempted murder of the East German, assault with a deadly weapon, assault on a foreign national, and assault on a member of the US Military, fleeing the scene, and failure to stop, resisting arrest, and carrying a weapon without authorization by a military court he was sentenced to thirty-five years. The East German survived the attack and testified at the court martial.

In July of 1994, a package, with an address from the eastern part of the recently unified city of Berlin, was delivered to the CID Special Agents, now housed at Clay Compound. In the package was a VHS cassette that contained the key evidence used to convict Herndez of the Premeditated Murder of PFC David Vela in his second trial. This time the sentence was life.

I never found out why he did it. I do not think he even knows. I guess he was used to getting what he wanted and when Vela's wife would not give him what he wanted, he took matters into his own hands. At the second trial, it was good to see Agents Emmett and Walter, again. Special Agent Ernest Walter retired a year after the Berlin Wall came down. Special Agent Manny Emmett is investigating criminal activity in Washington, D.C. this time as the lead agent for the entire United States Army Military District of Washington.

As for my roommates, Specialist David Brown went on to make a career out of the Army and the last time I heard he was back in Germany. Specialist Sean Wils left the Army and attended an Ivy League school where he got his law degree. As for Specialist Percival Ferriss, he got some medals and awards for his heroic actions that night at Checkpoint Charlie. Ferriss and I still get together once a year at his father's place in Oklahoma. Some years Wils joins us.

As for Ann and I. Well, we got married, moved to Texas, had two wonderful kids, and on November 9, 2009 we came back to Berlin to celebrate the 20th anniversary of the fall of the Berlin Wall. This time we came to party.

ABOUT THE AUTHOR

He was born in Texas, but Army brat David Guerra was not destined to roam the Lone Star State all his life. His father led him and his family to various military posts, and it was during his childhood and teenage years that David's thirst for adventure and travel began.

No one was surprised when David joined the U.S. Army as an Infantryman. His first duty assignment put him at the tip of the Cold War spear, 110 miles inside communist East German territory, in West Berlin arriving in 1985.

In Berlin, David's view of the world changed – especially that of the U.S. military inside the Berlin Wall during the Cold War. No longer was he just along for the ride with his father's assignments. Instead, David was learning from great leaders and managers the skills, knowledge and wisdom that would be the foundation for his adult life long after leaving Berlin and the Army. David left Berlin in 1987.

David went on to work for the State of Texas as a network analyst and eventually became an IT department manager. While working for the state, David completed his Bachelor's and Master's degrees in Business Administration, having decided it was best to work at gaining experience before going to school. Those years of experience combined with his education made David ready to deploy in the private sector. Now, he is in a position to influence not only his staff, but also everyone he encounters, on the path to becoming better individuals and leaders.

Doughboy City is David's second book but his first work of fiction.

David and his wife, Teresa, are proud of their children, Emma and Matthew, and they love to travel back to Berlin whenever possible.

David is online just about any time:
- twitter.com: @daveguerra
- http://www.facebook.com/pages/Dave-Guerra/286363668110733
- http://www.linkedin.com/profile/view?id=1095097
- http://www.daveguerra.com
- http://www.berlinbrigade.com

Made in the USA
Middletown, DE
22 June 2023

33234883R00064